A Fairytale or Not

A Fairytale or Not

Philip Badger Greenwood

authorHOUSE®

AuthorHouse™
1663 Liberty Drive
Bloomington, IN 47403
www.authorhouse.com
Phone: 1-800-839-8640

© 2011 by Philip Badger Greenwood. All rights reserved.

No part of this book may be reproduced, stored in a retrieval system, or transmitted by any means without the written permission of the author.

First published by AuthorHouse   07/27/2011

ISBN: 978-1-4567-8891-9 (sc)
ISBN: 978-1-4567-8892-6 (hc)
ISBN: 978-1-4567-8893-3 (ebk)

Printed in the United States of America

Any people depicted in stock imagery provided by Thinkstock are models, and such images are being used for illustrative purposes only.
Certain stock imagery © Thinkstock.

This book is printed on acid-free paper.

Because of the dynamic nature of the Internet, any web addresses or links contained in this book may have changed since publication and may no longer be valid. The views expressed in this work are solely those of the author and do not necessarily reflect the views of the publisher, and the publisher hereby disclaims any responsibility for them.

CONTENTS

1 Introduction
2 Uncle Asasta
3 Look back to the oak
4 The forester
5 Doorway to Paradise perhaps!
6 Visitor
7 Mound
8 The gift
9 What future mankind
10 Bonnie
11 Murphy's Law
12 Mermaid
13 I will not accept it
14 Freddie Chambers and Co
15 End message

A FAIRYTALE OR NOT DEDICATION

I dedicate this book to my dear wife and best friend to whom my heart will always belong. To all those that I hold close to my heart on earth and in heaven, and to you, that believe.
P B G

INTRODUCTION

Many a year has past since the day of my birth suffice to say that I am as old as my heart and as young as the winter snow. Odd that I should mention the winter for it was the season that I entered this world and it is my favourite. I love the magic of the season and the good will of the human spirit. It has always been this way with me and I shall never differ. My life differs none other that yours excepting perhaps that I have witnessed many a phenomenon. For example, spirits of the dead have visited and spoken with me. I have stood in my garden at night and watched unidentified flying objects cross the sky and disappear in the blinking of an eye. Moreover, yes. I have even seen a fairy. I live deep in the countryside and often feel the magic of the fairy folk around me. Not to long ago, I found myself driving down the long narrow road that eventually leads to my home. I was half a mile from my property and travelling at approximately 25 miles per hour. I have to pass a small coppice at the side of the road that boasts a mound in its centre. Perhaps it was from out of this mound that a little man appeared, I cannot say. However, of a sudden, a little man with beautiful transparent wings attached to his back, flew across my window screen. I must admit that these sightings are so very rare and that to witness such a sight is magnificent indeed. It has never accorded me to put my experiences to paper. However, after my last encounter with some very odd creatures, I have decided to give record of a few. My reason for this is that after you have read these few examples, perhaps you would care to read some of the following tales that I have accumulated over a period of many years. If after reading the first page of this book, you find yourself bah bahing. I suggest that you read no further. This book is not for you. However and if on the other hand you find that you cannot turn your face away from the page, read on, Enjoy. I had a very happy upbringing; therefore, I had no reason to fear neither any person nor anything. I have given you this fact and you will understand why after you have read the next few lines. My first experience with the paranormal was when I was knee high to a grasshopper. It was early morning and as I lay awake on the top of my bed sheets, I distinctly heard the sound of the water closet in use. A few moments later, I watched my bedroom door open wide and then close. I then heard footfalls crossing the room toward me until they reached the side of my bed. I looked down to the floor and saw a pair of blue feet disappear underneath it. I popped my head over the side and peeked. However, I was to be disappointed for I saw not an iota. At the breakfast table, I mentioned my experience. Of course, who would believe a six-year-old child when he states that he has seen the feet of his guardian angel? At the age of ten years, I was to continue with my education in a boarding school situated in the city of Birmingham some two hundred miles from my home in Essex. There, I was to reside for a period of five years, and can honestly admit that those five years were my happiest up until I met my dear wife of today. However, I had a detestation for the room I had been allocated. You see, a grotesque creature from the fifteenth century was still in residence and persisted in haunting me from the first day I entered the room and up until I left, five years later. In fact, when I first met the phantom Edgar, the very sight of him very nearly gave me free chocolate in my underpants. On the first night of taking to my bed, I was not long asleep when of a sudden; the sound of rustling in my bedside locker awoke me. I opened my eyes and found the room to be awash in an orange glow. In addition, standing by the side of my bedside locker was the most grotesque spectre I had hoped never to meet. Standing no more than four feet in hight was a skeleton covered in a grey skin; the creature wore about his body some filthy peasant rags that I presumed to be at least three hundred years old. He continued to stand by my bedside locker with one eye fixed on my person. The other eye was missing and in its place was a black void. The hair on his head was nothing but a mass of thick unkempt filth, and on his feet, he wore not a stitch. He lifted his left hand and pointed a bony finger toward me. With his other hand, he put his forefinger deep up his right nostril. Although I was very nearly shitting bricks, I refused to show any sign of fear, and so I asked him if he was enjoying his late supper? At the remark I made toward him, he became outraged. He screamed and hollowing to such an extreme, it was a wonder that the housemaster had not come running to my room, if only to find out what the entire racket was. However, he did not, and never did in all the five years that I was to reside there. The spectre screamed

"Who be you? Why be you in me bed?"

"What?"

"You be deaf? Me say who be you and why you be in me bed?"

"My name has nothing to do with you, and, I am in the bed that was allocated me when I first entered this house. In any case, have you looked at yourself lately? Do you not realize that you have been dead these past three centuries?"

"Of course, me knows. What you take me for, an idiot?"

"Yes, I believe you to be an idiot. What on Earth stopped you from entering through the light when first you died?"

"Venge".

"Sorry, I do not understand. What is venge?"

"Me wants venge before me goes in light"

"On whom?"

"That piece of shit that put pillow on me head"

"How do you expect to avenge your death? The person that murdered you has also been dead these past three hundred years"

"Nah, nah. You dun understand. We was friends 'til he finks it was funny to stick pillow on me head. Kills me, dun he. Me swears me dun go in light 'til me gets venge. To late for me now, init?"

"I can help if you please?"

"Dun be daft. How you help me?"

"I am a Christian. I can pray to God and ask him to release you from the bonds that hold you on Earth and to reunite you with yours ancestors"

"Nah. Me is in none for that sort of stuff"

Well. I will not bore you with the five years of continued haunting that I had to endure excepting the telling of my final parting with the miserable retch. It was early morning when my unwanted companion interrupted my sleep. He knew that this would be his last chance in tormenting me. Fool that I had been; I had told Edgar the night before that I should be leaving the school for good on the following day. It was no later than four in the morning when I felt a heavy weight on my chest and a putrid stench reached my nostrils. I awoke to find Edger my tormentor of the past five years, sitting astride my chest with his ugly face no less than an inch form my own.

"So, you be leaving today then?"

"I told you so last night, after you decided to keep me awake until close to midnight. Now get of my chest you filthy little devil"

"What you do if me dun? You cannot hurt me, me be dead"

"I will do something all right you dirty little stink bomb. These past few months I have been collecting earth from around the grave that your bones have been resting these past few centuries. Yes, my smelly friend, I have been reading up on unwanted visitors such as you. I have some of the earth under my pillow. All I have to do is throw some of it over you. Your ancestors will appear and take you away with them. By force if necessary"

"You would dare?"

"Yes, I would dare"

"You be a worm from the centre of your mother's gut. You think to afraid me. Cat vomit, Dog shit" "You can insult me as much as you wish Edgar. However, it will not stop me from sending you where you should have gone three hundred years ago. Now, get off me. You smell like an old shit tank"

At last, I felt his weight lift from my chest and the stench departed my nostrils. However, he spoke his final words to me as he climbed from the bed.

"You will regret your threat upon me for the rest of your life. You bag of horse shit"

His vile site no longer offended my eyes. In addition, I have never regretted my threat upon Edgar, yet, perhaps I should have, for over the past years, I have had to endure the many wrongs that have bestowed themselves upon my person. Still. I have not the right to make complaint because I have enjoyed my long life. In addition, I will continue to do so even on the day that I should depart this world and enter into the realm of the spirits, where I shall again be with my loved ones and the wonderful animals that I have known in this life and shall know in the next. On leaving the school of my education, I returned to my parental home and was not long in finding employment in a large food-processing factory.

However, I could not settle into this work and was soon on my way to the capital where I was most pleased in finding work. Also thanks to a colleague, I found a home with her and her family. My colleague, friend and landlady owned a seventeenth century house that contained four floors. In addition, to enter the front door, one had need to climb a flight of stone steps. My landlady had a grown family of which, most, had left home to start families of their own. Therefore, the top of the house was no longer in use. My landlady showed me up to the top floor where I was told to pick one of the many rooms for myself. Of course, I chose the largest and was most pleased that I should have the use of all the furnishings and any other requirements. The furnishings included a wardrobe that reached the ceiling and stretched the full eighteen feet width of the room with a four-foot in-depth. Had it could speak; it should have told many a secret for it was as old as the house that it occupied. At the other end of the room and standing under a window that should have allowed the entrance of a full-grown bull elephant, was an almighty king sized double bed. There also stood a chest of many drawers. In addition, lost in one corner of the room, there stood an old grand piano. Finely, the flooring was carpet covered. It was in this room that I was to meet and befriend my next apparition. I was not in residence for more than a few days when one evening whilst resting on the top of my bed reading A Christmas Carol by Charles Dickens. The bed started to sway from left to right. At the start, I hardly felt any swaying until of a sudden; it shook so violently, it was a wonder I was not thrown of the thing. I do believe that had the window been open, I should have enjoyed a flying lesson. However, and lucky for me, the window had not been opened for many a year. I jumped off the bed and saw standing at its foot, the misty appearance of a female. As each second went its way, the body of the female became more solid until finally I could see every detail. Accustomed, as was I to the seeing of phantoms, not in the whole of my body did I suffer an inkling of fear. I walked toward the female with my hand outstretched, ready to take hers in welcome. However, as our hands met, they passed through one another's as if they were a mist forming in a graveyard.

"Hello, my name is Philip. May I ask of you?"

She did not answer my greeting but, put her hand to her throat where I saw a gash so wide and deep, it was a wonder that she stood before me with her head still attached to her torso. With her long brown wavy hair, she stood five feet and six inches tall. In addition, adorned around her beautiful frame, she wore a long silk red dress that met with the prettiest of shoes. Had I had known better, I would have sworn that she was a fairy princess that had popped out of a book. I tried to talk with her again, but with that wicked gash in her neck, there was most certainly no way in which she had voice. However, within a few short weeks, she had taught me the rudimentary of sign language. Therefore, for more than a year, on the nights that my spiritual friend visited with me, we had at least a method of communicating with one another. I never mentioned the meetings that I enjoyed with my phantom friend to my landlady nor any members of her family because, they had immigrated to this country from the beautiful Caribbean islands early nineteenth century, and I knew them to be very superstitious. In addition, I had no wish to put the fear of God into their souls. My friend and I enjoyed many a night in the company of the other and had many entertaining discussions yet; she would never tell me how she had come about with that horrific gash in her throat. Moreover, she would not tell me until the last night of my residence in the property. I explained to her that I should be leaving on the following morning to return to my parental home for yet another short stay. I had no idea that new adventures in the paranormal, would eventually lead me into the writing of this book. That final night in the home of my landlady, I would not stop my persistent questioning of my friend until she gave into me, and gave her story.

* The next words that you will read are from the mouth of my friend and only quoted to memory *

"My father was a high ranking member of Parliament, so we were quite an aristocratic family. We never went short for wants and were very happy until my uncle came to stay and live with us. It was not long before I noticed that he and my mother were never far apart. It was also not long before I became suspicious that there was more than friendship between them, especially when my father was away from home and they believed me to be either in my rooms or away from the house. On the eve of my death, I was sitting in one of the high back lounge chairs that were facing away from the door, thus making me invisible from anyone that should enter the room. My uncle, my mother's lover, and she, entered the library, and thinking me to be away; they sat in the cosy chairs by the hearth and spoke freely. My uncle told my mother that he had arranged for his associates to enter into my father's office for the reason of taking away with them genuine papers, only to replace them with false papers that would discriminate my father. My mother and her lover were laughing at the thought of the constable calling at the house to take my father away to spend a considerable amount of time in the tower before his time of execution. They planed that my mother should visit the tower for asking a divorce because she could not stand by her husband knowing him to be a traitor. Enraged, I sprang from out of my chair ready to confront them for their planed evil deed. However, I had not the strength to keep them from off my person. My mother held me down upon the flooring whilst my uncle took from out of his scabbard an evil looking long knife and slit my throat from ear to ear. They then put my corpse into a secret compartment in that very wardrobe. It has never been disturbed".

She pointed to the wardrobe that I had been using for many months not knowing it to contain the remains of my companion. The spirit then drifted over to the great doors that swung open on her approach. Turning to face me, she beckoned me to follow her into the blackness. I followed my friend into the wardrobe thinking that I should have reason to strike a match so that I could see my way. However, I had no need because my friends form produced a mysterious but pleasant light plenty enough for my eyes. I followed my spiritual friend until she came to a stop and pointed to a knot high above her head. I reached up, pressed my finger against the knot and then watched in astonishment. A secret door of not more than three feet in hight and eighteen inches wide clicked open to reveal a small three foot by three-foot room. I had plenty headroom to enter and find sitting with her back to the wall, the remains of a young female wearing a red silk dress. All of a sudden, a beam of light appeared from the roof of the wardrobe and down upon my friend. However, before the light took her away, she looked me straight in the eyes and smiled. She told me that in years to come, she and I would meet again in Gods Kingdom. She was then heavenward lifted. Yes, there is many a tale that I could share with you that for some unknown reason I have been involved. For example, not to long ago, I met a man no taller than a wineglass. Alternatively, there was the time that I was invited entrance into the home of some very distinguished people. However, that is one story I made promise not to tell. Anywise, it is not my intention of writing this book giving only an account of my experiences. I have mentioned that over the past many years, I have collected a vast library. It is from this library that I have selected a small number of stories of which have infatuated me since infancy. I have chosen these stories because they are for not only the young but also the young at heart, the adventurers and the fear seekers. However, be forewarned. Some of these stories are not for the faint at heart. If you are reading this book for the first time, I envy you greatly because when I pick it up to read, I know what to expect. You on the other hand, do not.

Are the stories true?

A fairytale or not begins.

A FAIRYTALE OR NOT

Uncle Asasta

History informs us that the mountains of Kaff encircle our world, and living on these mountains are evil spirits. They are fire formed and are called Djinn. You have no doubt read the Arabian tale titled The Genie of the lamp. Moreover, have thought the story to be nothing but a fairytale. I can say without any hesitation that the storyteller of the time had read his history books and found that the mythical Djinn did and indeed do exist. It was this fact that prompted the teller of stories to write the tale of which is read all over the globe today. Although fire formed, the Djinn have the ability to change form at will to anything they wish excepting the flesh and bones of man. However, if the Djinn so wished, they can transform themselves into some resemblance of mankind but of portentous hideousness. The Djinn, it must be told, were given life many millenniums before man. For this reason, they believed themselves to be all-supreme. This fact reminds me of the filth that tortured and murdered millions of innocent people for pleasure. We called these evil monstrosities Nazis. However, I would like to claim that in all races, there are good and evil. God made man in his image and forbade the Djinn entrance to the world of his people because he knew that the Djinn would do just as did the Nazis during the middle twentieth century. Living there mortal lives on Kaff, the Djinn would not be content because they are a bloodthirsty race with no emotions other than hatred of mankind. Therefore, they were forever on the look for an escape from Kaff and entrance into this our world where they would cause such havoc that man in a thousand years will tell tales so horrifying, that when they retire to their beds, they will sleep trembling. In a land hidden from humanity, there is forest mass off 4000 square miles. In addition, there is not one tree in the forest, which has a girth of less than 40 feet and a hight of not less than 80 feet. On both sides of the forest and in its front, is a sea of ice and snow that is many thousands of miles before sight of any land. It is known to mankind as Antarctica. On the rear side of the forest, there is a land of lush green field as far and as wide as is the forest. On the far side of the field, there you will come upon the mountains of Kaff. On the mountains of Kaff lives a horde of monsters known as the Djinn. Fortunatley for the human race, one genie holds in his chest a heart of gold. Only this genie had the knowledge and wisdom to visit the forest, meet and befriend the little people and become the saint that he is known by today. His name at the time this story begins was Uncle Asasta. Today, he is proud to call himself by a different name. However, I will not redeem his new name until the end of this tale. Uncle Asasta was also the only genie that could transform himself perfectly into the flesh and bone of any four footed beast, he refused to become the image of man due to the fact that even he could not master the transformation. Had he tried, he would have become a mountain of! Well, you will find out soon enough. Therefore, on his visits to the little people, Uncle Asasta always arrived as a beast of the forest, a grizzly brown bear.

"Top of the day to you Uncle Asasta, What may I ask brings you to the forest today?"

"Greetings upon you Chieftain Wolftoes Fizelwing, I have come bringing grave news. My lord and master Growthead Dungball has come upon the pathway that I take from the mountains of Kaff. Eventually the pathway will lead him to the field and subsequently the forest. It will be only a matter of time before he and his great horde of fiends will find their way to the world of Eve's children. I have great strength and the ability to change form. Unfortunately, I do not have the magic of the forest dwellers. I can only hope and pray that you can stop Growthead Dungball in his wicked quest"

"Indeed Uncle Asasta. It is grave news that you have brought; yet still do I thank you. We have at least now the opportunity for preparations.

I shall call for an immediate meeting of the council. I pray that you have brought this news in time. I suggest that you return to your own kind other than your usual route for I fear that perchance, your lord and master should come upon you and force information from you as to the whereabouts of our home"

Uncle Asasta departed, leaving the chief of the forest dwellers to assemble the council and make plans for the forthcoming invasion of the Djinn. It was decided that an invisible wall was to be built and made from the minerals from the soils of the planet. The wall was to be built in the vast field one mile from the edge of the forest. It was to be built one mile high and one mile deep and it was to be built the full length of the forest. A four foot by four-foot passageway was to be permitted for the benefit of Uncle Asasta should he seek entrance into the forest. In addition, to stop any entrance by any undesirables, the passage was to be blocked with the entwined bones of the dead. The bones were to be soaked in one thousand drops of blood given freely by the unicorns that roamed the forest. In addition, the action of free blood running would not be enough. It was also required of the oldest unicorn in the forest to not only give a drop of blood but an incantation before freely giving his life so that a key should be fashioned from the dust of his bones and his blood fluids. He was to die in agonies and yet give no voice. In addition, whilst this beautiful creature was to suffer all these agonies, a keeper of the key was to be chosen. The key keeper was to be housed in the great oak that had stood on the very edge of the forest since the first seeds were sown many millenniums before. Finally, the passageway was to be built opposite and in full view of the great oak and the key keeper. In addition, all this work was to be completed no later than midnight that very night because if Growthead Dungball as said, should force information from Uncle Asasta. He would have his horde of monsters fighting the forest dwellers soon after. Fortunately, the magic of the forest dweller is very powerful thus; the task their chieftain had asked of them caused no hardship what so ever. Moreover, all had been completed in the time requested. In addition, whilst all this work was in progress, the name of the key keeper had been chosen. However, he had not been told of his new position because the moment he had completed the work asked of him, he had returned to his small abode in the middle of the forest where he had been experimenting with a new spell. When Wolftoes Fizlewing had seen that the task had been completed, he called the forest dwellers unto him.

"My fellow forest dwellers. It has been very difficult for the council in the choosing of the key keeper because each one of you has qualities unsurpassed. However, the members of the council have agreed that Paddlefoot Rattail will be asked to take upon himself this commision until the ending of time"

All eyes flashed from one dweller to another however, Paddlefoot Rattail was not to be seen. Wolftoes Fizelwing called out

"Is Paddlefoot amongst us?"

A hand shot up from the middle of the crowd.

"Yes, you there Tightlip Raspbutt. Have you seen our Paddlefoot?"

"No I have not Chieftain Wolftoes Fizelwing"

"Then, what do you wish to say Tightlip?"

"Why has Paddlefoot Rattail got the job? What is so special about him? Lets face it; he is nothing but an idle layabout"

"I can answer your questions Tightlip by asking you, and all those of you that think the same as Tightlip. Who amongst you have departed the forest and entered into the world of humans? Yes Tightlip. That is why Paddlefoot Rattail is best suited for the post of the key keeper. He will never leave his post" Another hand shot up from the middle of the crowd.

"Chieftain Wolftoes Fizelwing. I believe I know where Paddlefoot Rattail could be. After we had completed the tasks allocated us, Paddlefoot did not realize that that you was going to call for this assembly. He told me that he wanted to get back to his own little job. He is trying to grow apples on the sleeping willow that stands near to his small hollow"

"Thank you Butterfield Warmsnow. Will you please find your friend and inform him that his presence will be appreciated in the queen's chambers. It is most imperative that the gateway is entwined this night. Should Growthead Dungball chance upon Uncle Asasta, Information will be forced from him and all Hell will be upon the human race"

Before Wolftoes had finished his sentence, Butterfield was off like the wind to the hollow of her friend with pride written on her face. Her best friend was to be offered the most important job in the forest. Only will He, have the power to open and close the gateway of entwined bones. Whilst Butterfield was on her way to find her friend, Wolftoes was still standing amongst his fellow forest dwellers and talking at the top of his voice.

"Our work this day is compleat. I must say that as usual, you have all!"

Bucktooth Blackfeet had not heard a single word spoken all evening because his ears were full of earwax that he needed to add to other ingredients he had put together for a spell he had been working on for some months.

"Why has Paddlefoot Rattail been offered this most important job Chieftain Wolftoes Fizelwing?"

"Because Bucktooth Blackfeet, Paddlefoot Rattail is one of the oldest gnomes living in the forest, His age is more than three time one thousand years and yet, not once has he asked entrance into the world of the humans. Can anyone here say the same?"

Not a murmur was heard from the gathering of many.

"As usual, you have all shown and given exceeding willingness in what you have performed this day. I can only thank you and wish you all an exceedingly superb evening"

Butterfield found Paddlefoot where she had expected. He was standing at the foot of the weeping willow pouring a sickly green liquid over its bark and shouting incantations toward it. However, to his disappointment, there was no fruit.

"Hello Butterfield. No success I'm afraid"

"Paddlefoot, if only you had remained with the gathering on the compleation of the great wall"

"Why Butterfield, what happened?"

"Wolftoes sent me to tell you that at this very moment, the council are assembled and awaiting your presence in the chambers at the queen's palace"

She was so proud of what her best friend was to become that she had to tell him before anyone else. "Paddlefoot, you have been chosen to be the keeper of the key"

"Why has the council chosen me Butterfield?"

"I do not know Paddlefoot. Best be off to the palace. You will be told all that you need to know there" Paddlefoot was up and running as the wind and at his side, was his best friend and future bride. When they arrived at the palace, they found two trolls guarding the entrance.

"Gordey masser Piddlefeet, You be spected. Gorin, bah you Miss Bitterroot, you gor stay ear and whey wif us"

Both Paddlefoot and Butterfield understood the language of the trolls and did as been told them. Paddlefoot entered through the entrance and into the great hall where he was greeted by yet another troll, this time slightly smaller than the two guarding the entrance. However, he had developed a few more brains than his fellows had. It was for this reason that he had been accepted inside the palace. "Welcome Master Paddlefoot, you are expected. Please follow me"

He took Paddlefoot down the long hallway until they arrived at a door where he abruptly stopped forcing Paddlefoot to walk smack bang into his trunk like legs.

"Please wait here whilst I introduce you to the council Master Paddlefoot"

With a fist the size of a beach ball, the troll banged twice on the door and then entered.

"Your chieftain Sir, Master Paddlefoot is waiting outside the door"

"Thank you Throttle, Please ask him to enter and then you can go about your duties"

Holding Paddlefoot by the scruff of the neck, Throttle ushered Paddlefoot into the room and pushed him into a seat in the corner.

"You will wait here until you have been called Master Paddlefoot"

Paddlefoot shot an angry look toward Throttle.

"I am not here because I have commited a wrong doing Throttle"

"Perhaps not Master Paddlefoot but I am not to know that am I?"

Although Chieftain Wolftoes Fizzlewing was immerged in conversation with the council members, he also heared Paddlefoot shouting and looked over to his key keeper to see that he was being held by the scruff. He stood up and in an authoritative voice called out

"Throttle, You have been employed in the policing of this palace, however. I believe your head to be large enough. There is no need for you to show of your authority. You know why Paddlefoot Rattail has been asked to attend this council chamber. You may go about your business now. Thank you"

Throttle felt embarrassed. All he wanted now was the floor to open up so that he could disappear beneath it. Ashamed and embarrassed, he appoligised and left the room.

"Top of the day to you Paddlefoot, Are you well?"

"Yes thank you Chieftain Fizzlewing"

"Paddlefoot, when we are at council, we are not at all ceremonious. You may call me by my first name, Wolftoes. Have you been advised as to the reason why you have been summonsed to this meeting?" "Yes Wolftoes. Butterfield Warmsnow told me that you want me to be the keeper of the keys"

"Slightly wrong there Paddlefoot. We do not want you to be the keeper of the keys. We wish you to be the keeper of the key. The key that I speak of has been fashioned from the bones of the dead and has been blessed with one drop of blood from every unicorn that roams freely in the forest. However, there are still a few unsavoury things that I must do before it has the power to either entwine and or release the bones in the gateway"

"Why should we wish to release the bones Wolftoes?"

"Because Paddlefoot. On the occasions that Uncle Asasta should seek entrance into the forest, you will have need to release the gate of bones. You must remember Paddlefoot that Uncle Asasta will appear as he has done so, these many years. He will appear as a brown grizzly bear. Before you open up the gateway, Uncle Asasta will speak these words. The gardens of Leazlock are ashen these days. If he speaks other than these words to you, you will not open up the gateway. After he has spoken these words, you will reply, Yes, however the seeds of Glorysands will satisfy. Even then, you must wait for his reply. He will say, Then let the waters run free"

Paddlefoot looked puzzled and asked his chieftain

"Why do we have to go through all this paraphernalia Wolftoes?"

"Because Paddlefoot, as far that we know, Uncle Asasta is the only Genie who can transform himself into a flesh and bone body; now, what do you think would happen to the human race if Growthead Dungball found the formula in performing the same?"

Paddlefoot knew that his question had been rather stupid and apologised.

"Apology accepted Paddlefoot. Now, once you have accepted Uncle Asasta to be the genuine article, you will put the key to your lips and speak the words that will release the entwined bones I.E. the gateway. I will give these words to you when we have gone through the passageway and are in the field"

"May I ask why we have need to enter the field Wolftoes?"

"Because Paddlefoot. There are but two creatures permitted the knowledge to these words that will either set the bones to hold, or become dust"

"There is just one final question if you will permit Wolftoes?"

"Ask your question Paddlefoot"

"The wall travels the width of the forest. It is one mile high, and as deep. What I would understand from you please is, when our friend Uncle Asasta should seek entrance through the gateway. How will I hear the other speak?"

"Paddlefoot, There are times I would say that your brains are as thick as your beard. Are we not the sprite of the forest? Was not the magic of the Elfin given to us when last they made visit more than a millenium before this day?"

"Once again, I thank you Wolftoes for making a fool such as I, understand"

"Come Paddlefoot, it is time for us to take the walk through the gateway and onto the field"

Chieftain Wolftoes Fizzlewing and the keeper of the key bade the council a goodnight and departed the palace. They headed for the mile high wall, entered though the gateway and walked the mile distance to the field on the other side. As they reached the halfway mark, Paddlefoot noticed that his chieftain had need to wipe his eyes many times.

"You are greatly saddened Wolftoes. May I ask the reason?"

"Yes Paddlefoot, I am greatly saddened. I am afraid that there is a little more that I need to tell. I should have told you before but I could not bring myself to say anymore at that time. Earlier I told you that there are just two creatures permitted the knowledge of the words that will free or entwine the bones. I am saddened because the very moment you receive the knowledge, one of the others will give up his life. Our friend, the oldest unicorn in the forest will impale himself onto a wooden stake. He will remain there until his last drop of blood has fed this thirsty earth. The spirit will then depart the shell and roam free in Paradise forever. I will return to my humble abode where I shall continue in the performing of my duties until such time that I to shall enter Paradise. For you, a home has been fashioned in the great oak that stands on the edge of the forest and opposite the gateway of entwined bones"

Wolftoes looked up to the heavens and called out

"Until we met again prince Wunchonite"

Then with tears freely falling from his eyes, Wolftoes Fizzlewing gave to Paddlefoot Rattail a string of words.

"When you have need to speak these words Paddlefoot, speak them loud and clear. Now listen carefully. To open the gate, you have need to put the key to your mouth and kiss it. Then must you speak before the ending of the twntieth second, for if you do not; your bones will be added to those that bar entrance to all uninvited visitors. Emeidatly after you have kissed the key, you will say, Friend Wunchonite. Inprint your heart blood here. You will see the key change colour from bone to gold, the same colour as unicorn blood. You will then face the gateway, put the key to your mouth and softly blow over it toward the gate of entwined bones. The moment you have used up your intake of air, you will again put the key to your mouth and kiss it. To close the gateway, you will perform the same actions excepting that you will speak other words. These words shall be, Friend Wunchonite. I return to you your heart blood until I have need of it again. After you have kissed the key for the final time, you will see that it will change colour from gold to bone. These duties will be all that is required of you until you either choose no longer to be the keeper of the key, or another key holder has been chosen by the council"

Wolftoes gave the key to Paddlefoot and then pointed toward the forest to which they both returned. When they arrived back inside the safty of the forest, Wolftoes bade a goodnight to his key keeper and went his way. Paddlefoot put the key to his mouth, said a string of words and then turned to face the invisible wall. Again, he put the key to his mouth and blew over it toward the gateway, he then kissed it and watched as a pile of dust covering the full length of the passageway become a mass of entwined bones. The key returned to the colour bone as he put it inside his purse, and the purse he put deep inside his jacked pocket. He then turned to face his new home inside the great oak of which was a substantial difference to his former home. The mortals were now free from the evil Djinn and would remain so for many thousands of years because the forest dwellers were there to protect them. Forest dwellers differ from you and I. Fairy folk are immortal. As to the gate of bones. They are the remains of the human beings that lived in unison with the forest dwellers and whos bones were buried deep beneath the forest leaves. I would also point out at this time that when the forest dwellers asked a droplet of blood from every unicorn of the forest, they asked so because unicorns are creatures of purest of pure whereas, men commit sin on a daily basis even when they try not. For example. A man that has plenty yet still envies the wealth of another. The unicorn's blood was impregnated into the bones of the dead. Only then could the magic required of the gateway come into force. The moment the bones were entwined, they would permit not an evil spirit entry. In fact, if an evil spirit attempted entry, the vile thing would be thrown a thousand miles from the wall. It was also impossible for the Djinn to climb the invisible wall because it is as a sheet of still waters. Fire can neather climb nor hurt nature's minerals. In addition, with all the enchantments that the foreat dwelleres put upon the wall, not one fiend would dare attempt entrance. At the first, Paddlefoot was very happy in his new home and enjoyed his high-ranking job as the key holder. However, after weeks had turned into months and month into years and many centuries had passed by, he began to feel that surly there was much more to life and that he could be doing something more constructive than just sitting in his rocking chair and watch the gateway everyday. Fair enough, he was married to his beautiful Butterfield and had every comfort he could possibly want. Yet still, he was truly bored until one day, whilst sitting in the new rocking chair he had built on the new porch he had also built, and again complaining as usual of his boredom, Growthead Dungball had found the pathway that would eventually lead him to the world of his enemies, mankind. He had travelled across the land of field and come up against the invisible wall. He sped up along it one way and then the other until he came upon the gateway. However, the moment he tried to push his way through the entwined bones, a force he had never known before threw him back to the mountains of Kaff. It was good that Paddlefoot had heeded the words of his chieftain because, within a few moments of his flight back to Kaff, Growthead Dungball had returned to the gateway disguised as a giant rooster. Paddlefoot sat comfortably in his rocking chair looking amusingly at the rooster who was at this time striding to and thro and looking to be quite frustrated at the predicament, he found himself to be in. Finally, he called out to the little twerp sitting and watching him outside his door in the old tree.

"Pardon my pressence little friend. Please allow me to pass through the bones and enter the forest".

The gnome could hardly contain his laughter when he answered in as serious a note he could muster. "What's the password?"

Dungball had great difficulty in keeping his temper.

"I do not have the password; I have been kept a prisoner in the land of the Djinn these past twenty years. Please allow me return to my home in the great forest"

Paddlefoot burst into an uncontrollable laugh that took sometime before he finally calmed down to speak.

"Do you really think me as stupid as your kind Growthead Dungball? I have seen many roosters but never have I seen one the hight of a ten-ton pile of poo. Go away Dungball and try another day. By the way, Thanks for the good laugh"

Growthead Dungball was not in the least pleased with the answer he had received from the keeper of the key and before he turned his back on the still laughing gnome, he called back

"You piece of fairy shit. Do you really think to keep me out? I will return with my fellow Djinn to teach you filth, a lesson or two"

Paddlefoot took not a hair notice of the monster's threat but continued to sit in his chair still laughing and waving to Dungball as he disappeared into the distance. Paddlefoot had taken not the slightest notice of Dungball's threat until the following spring. Although he had the most important job in the forest, he occasionally was permitted to take a break from his duties. Therefore, he and Butterfield had gone off visiting their friends for the day when. On their return to the oak, they saw that the field on the other side of the wall had sprouted a countless number of shrubs. He did no more but went off to consult his sightings to his chieftain. However and unfortunately, the one forest dweller Paddlefoot had no desire to see was a gnome called Furbungle Lightstar. As far that he could remember, He and Furbungle had no liking for the other ever since Furbungle had stole a spell book from Paddlefoots home of which had taken Paddlefoot many years to compleat. Paddlefoot had actually seen the guilty party doing the wicked deed, and although he had reported the theft, Furbungle Lightstar insisted the book to be his own work. In fact, it was for this reason Wolftoes Fizzlewing took it upon himself to take Furbungle as his fulltime assistant. Wolftoes had guessed the truth and he was not going to give the thieving gnome another chance. In addition, Wolftoes had introduced a new law in that no forest dweller was to keep record of their spells.

"Good evening Paddlefoot Rattail. May I require the reason of your visit to the dwellings of Chieftain Wolftoes Fizzlewing?"

"You can ask until the ending of days Furbungle Lightstar, however, I will never give you a true answer. It is enough that you know, I seek my chieftain"

Furbungle Lightstar knew his adversaey would give nothing away and that Paddlefoot had office over him. He had no choice but to allow Paddlefoot into his chieftain's abode. They entered into a large oval room lined with comfortable chairs and a large oval table in its centre. Furbungle invited Paddlefoot into one of the chairs close by the door they had just entered through and told him in an authoritative voice to remain there until his return. Furbungle Lightstar was not gone for more than a minute when he returned and asked the key keeper to enter through the only other door in the cavern. This was the office and the living quarters of their chieftain. Paddlefoot nodded to Furbungle Lightstar and then entered for the first time in his live the home of Wolftoes Fizzlewing. Wolftoes was sitting at his desk behind a mountain of paperwork.

"Top of the day to you Paddleffot, How may I be of assistance?"

"I apologise for my presence Chietain Wolftoes Fizzlewing. I believe you should know that the field beyond the wall has produced many thousands of unidentified shrubs"

"Ah! I have been expecting this for some time. All you can do for now Paddlefoot is to keep a close eye on the field and to let me know of any progress"

"May I ask of what you have been expecting Wolftoes?"

"I suspect that every shrub standing in the field Paddlefoot is in fact, a member of the Djinn"

Therefore, for more than a few centuries, Paddlefoot Rattail watched the growing of a great forest as massive and as beautiful as the forest he and his Butterfield had lived and loved all the days of their lives. In addition, for another two thousand years, they sat and watched the new forest grow such delicious and marvellous fruits that Mother Nature would be tempted to sample for herself. They both had to watch in disgust as the fruits ripened and fell to feed the maggots and other wriggling and crawling creatures on the ground underneath the whispering Djinn in their diguise as trees. Moreover, for more than two thousand years, their tormentors would not give up their temtations until Paddlefoot could hold his desires no longer. His enemies even gave promise of none interfearence should he wish to partake at his leisure of the bounteous fruits that had not touched the lips of a single fairy since first they grew on the trees in the new forest. However, Paddleffot and Butterfield knew not to trust a single word from the mouth of a genie and that any promise a genie makes, he will find no difficulty in breaking. "The Djinn make it so hard to resist Butterfield. I do so want to taste a delicious Lanbilberry, and just look at those scummy Scheels. And those Phatash berries are four times as large as any I have ever seen. Look at those Foamtips. I've just got to have one of them"

"Yes, yes, yes my Paddlefoot. That is all fine but you know that everyone of those trees is a member of the Djinn. How do you expect to collect the friut without getting caught?"

"I have a plan Butterfield. If I open the gateway and there is a sudden attack from the Djinn. I will emmediately close it even if it means that I should be trapped between the entwined bones. Anywise, should this happen. Wolftoes will no doubt find a way of releasing me and keeping out the Djinn" Paddlefoot took his way to the gateway, took out the key and performed a sequence of actions that reduced the bones to dust. He waited a while to see if there would be any undesirable actions from the Djinn and was pleased that there was none. He took the mile long walk through the passageway and stopped at its end where he performed the magic that returned the bones to their original position in that the gateway was again closed up as tight as a ducks bottom. He then took his way to the forest where he chose a particularly large tree that grew berries so huge; he found it difficult to hold just one in both hands. Unfortunatly, the genie showing itself to be a fruit tree, was none other than the monster, Growthead Dungball.

"Wow, this Phatash berry is going to take an effort to get back home"

"Do you really think so you foul smelling fairy"

When Paddlefoot heard these words, he saw that the Phatash berry he was holding in his hands had become a large, crusty, bogey. Moreover, the tree that he had taken the Phatash berry from had become a mountain of boils, scabs and oozing pus. in addition, as had their lord and master taken shape, so did the remaining hord become their true selves. Growthead Dungball looked down to the gnome smiling. "Let me relieve you of that weighty looking instrument you have in your hand my little friend"

"You are no friend of mine Growthead Dungball. I will not loose the key for the world"

Dungball knew that there was no way on earth he could hurt the gnome. However, he also knew that he could take the key away from Paddlefoot with ease. He took Paddlefoot up in his great pus filled hand. "Who is the one laughing now, turd face?"

However, Paddlefoot was undeterred.

"You cannot use the key Dungball. You have not the magic of the forest dwellers. Not including the chants, you also have to know what to do with the key, or all will go wrong for you"

"Is that so you filthy piece of slug shit? Well, let me guess"

The monster threw Paddlefoot hard against the invisible wall all the time watching the gnome eagle eyed should the gnome drop the key and, to where the key should fall. Of course, as is the norm, Sods law i.e. Murphy, was about his duties and forced the key from out of Paddlefoots hand. By the time the poor gnome was upon his feet; one of the Boil Mountains had taken it up and handed it to his master. Growthead watched in surprise as the key he held in the palm of his hand slowly but surly sized itself to that of a six foot mans shinbone. He kissed the key and then spoke.

"Friend Wunchonite imprint your heart blood here"

He then faced the gateway, put the key to his mouth and blew gently over it until he reached his breaths end. He kissed the key and then looked down to Paddlefoot laughing. The bones had become dust and the Djinn took the short journey through the passageway, through the home of the forest dwellers and onward to the world of mankind. Before entering through the portals of our world, the Djinn became invisible thus, many a time did they return to Kaff rejoicing their evil deeds. Then when lust for blood again reached their vile hearts did they return to the world of mankind forcing more suffering. Temptations were put upon powerful men and women causing them to war on others, thus murdering millions of innocents so as to fill their greedy fists with profits. Nourishment was taken from the earth and millions of innocents starved to their deaths. Corrupt governments all over the world became greedy giving false promises. And all the time, taking most everything for themselves whilst giving very little to the nations. Greedy businessmen and women bought up everything possible thus making it impossible for others to make a decent living. Greedy property developers destroyed beautiful green and pleasant lands to build unwanted concrete jungles. The more land these property developers could take, the more they wanted and as far as they were concerned. Dam the beautiful wild life that occupied these lands and forests. When the evil djinn had had enough, they returned to Kaff where they rejoiced their wicked deeds. Many a time did the Djinn return to the world of mankind. And many a time did they take pleasure in seeing the sufferings of their enemies. However, one jinni refused to enter the world of mankind. He knew that the living God had not only given life to the Djinn but that he gave life to all creatures on all worlds. And, as his God loves mankind, so should this jinni. However, Growthead Dungball believed that he and his horde were the all-powerful, supream intelligence throughout the universe. He had forgotten that his God was also the God of mankind. As far as he was concerned, He had the sole right to destroy all living creatures.

Liking blood thirsty men, women and children who enjoy the sufferings of wild animals that they hunt down to murder

Uncle Asasta was the jinni who refused to partake in the so-called pleasures of his kind. He refused to enter the world of mankind but abided his time until the day came when Growthead Dungball returned to the field and made the gateway of dust, bone. It had been a most pleasurable time for him and his horde. They had enjoyed putting perverted thoughts into the heads of men and women. They had enjoyed watching humans suffer death due to the acts of their perversions. And, they had set free the Imps, Goblins and Trolls to cause even more hardships on their enemies. At last, Uncle Asastas waiting had ended. Dungball and his filth had had such a good time that instead of returning to Kaff, they remaind in the field a while celebrating. Uncle Asasta watched his master as would an owl watch his victim before pouncing. Growthead was no more than a few yards from the gateway and did not relise that he had let loose the key. All Uncle Asasta had now to do was wait for the Djinn return to Kaff still boasting of the wicked deeds they played in the murdering of their human scum victims. The moment the field was empty; Uncle Asasta was upon the key, released the entwined bones, flew through the passageway and returned the dust to bone. He had been very lucky because, within a split second of closing the gateway forever, Growthead Dungball was on the otherside of the invisible wall shouting for Uncle Asasta return to his kind with the key that belonged to his lord and master. However, Uncle Asasta ignored the monster and changed form from the monster he was to the good old grizzle bear that the forest dwellers had known and loved many centuries. Paddlefoot and Butterfield were the first to greet him followed by Wolftoes and then the rest of the forest dwellers. Paddlefoot took the key from out of the mouth of the brown bear and handed it to Wolftoes but Wolftoes told him to keep the key. He was still the official key holder and no one could argue the fact.

"Top of the day to you Uncle Asasta. I cannot thank you enough for what you have done"

"Greetings Chieftain Wolftoes Fizzlewing. I have to tell you that it was not the fault of Paddlfoot Rattail that my fellow Djinn entered the world of humans. I only found out how Growthead Dungball knew the magic of the key after he had returned from his first killing spree. One of your own followed you when first you visited the field with Paddlefoot to give him instructions on how to use the key. Furbungle Lightstar used a spell he had stolen from a book in your own library that would make him invisible. He took note of the spell that should open and close the gateway. Then he left it by the gate for Growthead to find. All Furbungal had to do then was to follow you and Paddlefoot back through the passageway and then go about his duties as normal. Now that Paddlefoot has the key back, I will ask him what he intends to do with it"

"I only wish I knew Uncle Asasta. If you are going to where I suspect, may I ask that you take it away with you?"

For a long while, all was as quiet as the day, but of a sudden, a booming voice was heard.

"Yes Uncle Asasta. You take the key away with you. There is no doubt that you will return to your own kind someday, there is no doubt about that at all. And on that day, we shall enter through the gateway again. And, I can asure you Uncle Asasta and your little friends, that on that day, we shall take you along with us to enjoy the torturing of the human filth that pollutes this planet twenty-four hours a day. When we return to Kaff, Uncle Asasta. There will be not a single human living to tell the tale"

He ended his speech with a roudy laugh. Uncle Asasta nudged the key keeper and asked for the key of which Paddlefoot gave him with his chieftains blessing. He then turned to face Growthead making sure that Growthead saw the key between his teeth and then began to chew away until the key was nothing but a paste. After swallowing the paste, Uncle Asasta spoke his final words to the prince of the Djinn. "See what I have done to the key Dungball? I will be shortly leaving this world of magic to a place of my choosing, where I shall eventually shit out the key with the knowledge that not even my friends the forest dwellers will attempt repair. As far as I am concerned Dungball. You are nothing to me but a Dungball. You have always been so and you shall always remain so. Now be off with you"

Uncle Asasta and his friends the forest dwellers looked to see standing at the side of Growthead Dungball none other than Furbungle Lightstar. Dungball was furious. He attacked the passageway of entwined bones with all the force he could muster. However, He and his servant Furbungle Lightstar were thrown to a place that I dare not tell, for I fear that should you ever come upon an old oil lamp, you should set them free. The world was now free from the evil Djinn and would remain so for all eternity. Paddlefoot asked Uncle Asasta if he would journey to the place that Paddlefoot suspected.

"Yes my friend. I will travel to the place of ice and snow and find a home there where I shall remain until the end of days. Perhaps once in a daylight moon, I shall return to the forest for I feel that although I am a jinni, I have been accepted as a forest dweller"

The whole forest became alive with applause, laughter and joyous talk until Wolftoes Fizzlewing put up his hand and asked for quiet.

"Uncle Asasta. You are indeed a forest dweller. When one thousand years have past, we shall meet again with a gift that you have wished all the days of your life. Until then my friend, farewell"

Uncle Asasta left his friends and went his way through the forest and onto the coast. here, he changed form to that of a giant albatross and took flight across the vast seas until he came upon the island of ice and snow where he transformed himself a final time to that of a thick coated white bear. Now this is where you would think my story ends for it would seem that there is very little to tell. However, I am pleased to say that I have much more for you. Uncle Asasta did indeed stay on the island of ice and snow for more than a thousand years. And, for more than a thousand years did the forest dwellers have eyes upon him. One day whilst sitting at the side of a sea-lions air hole and talking to the owners who showed no fear of their natural enemy, a snow-fox approached and sat at his side.

"Many greetings upon you Uncle Asasta"

"Many blessings upon you Frixy. The look on your face tells me that you have something important to say?"

"Yes Uncle Asasta, Chieftain Wolftoes Fizzlewing has sent me to you"

"Did he really Frixy? I have missed all the chats that he and I had in secrecy all those years ago. Tell me, how is the old fart?"

"He has changed not an iota since last you and he spoke more than a millenium ago. He would have you meet with delegates from the forest; you may choose the time and place"

"Have you the authority to give me the reason for this meeting Frixy?"

"I can tell you that a proposal will be put before you. And, that if you accept the conditions of the proposal, not only will your life be changed for the better but that of the human race"

"Well Frixy, as it is also for the benefit of the human race. Of course, I will meet with the delegates. However Frixy, I believe that you know more than you tell"

"I do Uncle Asasta. However, it is up to the delegates to give you this information"

"Very well Frixy. You can inform the delegates that there is a village called Flowsten. It is sixty miles north from this air hole. I will be waiting twenty miles this side of the village at this time tomorrow" "Thank you Uncle Asasta. I can tell you that you will never regret your decision"

Frixy ran off into the far distance leaving Uncle Asasta and the sea lions he had been talking to; watch her until she was out of sight.

"I am so very sorry Mrs Nicktail. I would love to inform you and you family that you are safe from the hunger attacks of Mr Snorker. However, may I ask? How do you think the fish feel when you and your family fill your bellies on them?"

"That is an excellent point Uncle Asasta. I will say no more on the matter. Blessings upon you and until we meet again"

Mrs Nicktail returned to the safty of the waters leaving Uncle Asasta to begin his forty miles strech toward the village of Flowstem. And twenty-four hours later as promised, he found himself standing on the spot where he expected to meet with the delegates of the forest that he had known and loved all those years ago. He had only to wait a short while when he saw a small dark patch approaching and was soon to realize that it was not a group but a single delegate. To save the delegate a long walk, Uncle Asasta started a trot toward him and as they approached one another, the forest dweller lifted his right hand and put it upon the shoulder of the huge white bear.

"Hello Uncle Asasta. It is so nice to see you again after all this time. I left the others to wait for us at the village inn"

"It's good to see you also Paddlefoot Rattail. However, I dare not go into to the village. The villagers would chase me off with their spears unless I enter as my true form. Then, they would be running in the opposite direction never to return"

Paddlefoot denied Uncle Asastas statement and gave his reason.

"Uncle Asasta, when you told Frixy that you would meet with us for the benefit of the human race, you also lost your ability to transform yourself ever again. You are no longer a jinni but the bear that walks at my side. Uncle Asasta, for many thousands of years, you, have wanted to be as mankind. Look down upon yourself and see the man that you have become"

Whilst they had been walking the twenty miles toward the village of Flowsten, Uncle Asasta had very slowly changed form so that by the time they had reached the outskirts of the village he had changed form from the great white bear he had been for more than a thousand of years to that of a man dressed in furs, he had become a human being. And, when the two of them reached the village inn and the door was opened to them, Uncle Asasta became very joyous. Sitting at one of the larger tables that had been situated by a window away from prying eyes and ears were friends he had thought never to see again. Mrs Goatbeak was up and shaking his hands in hers before he had set foot inside the building and the door closed to shut out the icy cold.

"Uncle Asasta, How are you?"

"All the better for seeing you Wintip. My goodness, I have not forgotten any one of you here. Now let me see. Ah yes, Mr Leafgreen Rootsway, Mrs Wandsley Coalshoe, Mr Twiggle Pipsnoogle, Mr Fungi Grassqueek. Even you Mr Griptight Toadgruff. How I have missed each and every one of you"

After much hugging and shaking of hands, the friends eventually returned to the table by the window where glasses filled to the brim with the much-loved Phatash berry juice was put before them. Paddlefoot spoke.

"My friends. Now that we have rejoiced in the much-awaited reunion. And, with this wonderfully invented drink that has been put before our palates to enjoy. I suggest we put forward the proposal we have wished to put before Uncle Asasta for many thousands of years"

Everyone agreed and so with little ado Paddlefoot looked Uncle Asasta in the eyes and put forward the long awaited proposal.

"Uncle Asasta. How would you like to remain the man that sits at this table for all time?"

"I would like that very much Paddlefoot"

"Of course you would, of course you would Uncle Asasta. At the far end of this village do a young mother and her three small children occupy a cabin. Not long ago the man of this family went out hunting for meat. However, the very bear he had been hunting attacked and killed him. His family are desperate for food and warmth yet there is not a soul that will give. In a few moments, this young family will pass this inn. Go out and see them, but remember Uncle Asasta, you do not have the magic of the forest dwellers. However, please take these gold coins with you"

Uncle Asasta stood up pushing his seat away from him with the backs of his legs, walked over to the door, looked back to his friends and then disappeared into the cold night. He had not long to wait for the family he had been told about but, in the short time that he did wait, many people passed him by and all wearing furs from their heads to their toes. However, the family he had been waiting for could not be ignored as they passed him by. He saw that each of them had very little on their backs to keep out the bitter cold, and that the slippers on their feet had very little leather. The mother held her youngest child in her arms whilst her two elder children walked at her side. Uncle Asasta followed the fatherless family from a distance until they entered a small cabin at the very edge of the village. He waited until the door was shut before sneaking up to the cabin and peeking through the window. He could not stop the tears from rolling down his fat face as he watched the family sit down upon cold wood flooring around an old crate that had been turned so that the bottom had became the top of which, was used as a table. The table stood empty from any sustenance and as far as Uncle Asasta could tell, there was no food in the cabin what so ever. His face was now soaked with the tears that ran freely from his eyes. He pressed his face hard against the windowpane hoping for any sound of conversation.

"I am so hungry mother. Is there anything we can eat?"

"I am so sorry my darlings. There is not a crumb in the place. Perhaps we shall eat on the morrow" "Oh, I do hope so mother, my tummy hurts"

"I will collect your bedding my dears. Sleep will take the pain away"

She gave her child in arms to her eldest and then went into the only other room in the cabin shortly to return to her children with some bedding furs. She then took up her youngest and returned to the room she had just come out off. Before entering, she gave to her two eldest her blessings and then shut the door. Uncle Asasta crept around to the back of the cabin and took in another view through the window. The room contained another crate that was half the size of the one in the next room.

This crate was being used as a cot for her child. She had laid some furs on the inside and then her child whom she then covered with what remaining furs she possessed. She then lay down at the side of the cot with only the clothing she wore on her back and wept until she slept. Uncle Asasta put his hand into his pocket that held the coins he had been given, asking himself

"What is the worth of these coins? How long will they keep this poor family in food? I doubt very much that they will last for long before this family will suffer again"

He sat himself down by the side of the cabin and became a statue until of a sudden; he stood upon his feet and was off like the wind returning to the inn with all hope that it was still full with merry making souls.

"Landlord, what will these coins get me?"

"Bless you sir, they will get you this inn"

"I do not want your inn landlord. However, I would like to get everyone in your inn this night a drink" Well, you can imagine, after a couple of hours, Uncle Asasta was not only the talk of Flowsten but also the best friend of each soul in the village.

"Cheers Uncle Asasta"

"And the same to you Master Threebeans"

"How long can we enjoy your company Uncle Asasta?"

"I have no idea Madam Frustpaws. Perhaps I shall settle here"

"Will you really Uncle Asasta. I expect you will start a business here will you not?"

"I have no plans Mr Gravefoot. However, my friends, I have been in your village for a matter of a few hours and you have all, made me most welcome. Yet, at the far end of your village, there lives a young mother with her three small children. They have very little food in the cabin, if any. There is not a stick of furniture and, there is no fire in the hearth. They own very few furs for warmth. And, the floor that they sit and sleep is but cold wood. How long may I ask of you people, have you known this poor family?" When Uncle Asasta had begun his speech, the room had been awash with merry making people enjoying the drinks that had not lightened their purses a single farthing. However, after he had spoken just a few words in defence of the poor family, every head in the inn was hung in shame. The villagers left the inn. "A room for the night if you please landlord"

"Just the night Uncle Asasta?"

"Just the one night landlord"

Uncle Asasta decided that he would leave Flowsten at sunrise returning to his home some sixty miles away but before leaving, he would go the the cabin at the end of the village and hand over the remaing coins to the young mother. However, when he arrived at the cabin on the following morning, he had yet again to wipe tears from his eyes and this time, it was not due to sadness. The whole village had turned out crowding the cabin inside and out.

"By the Snowgobber convention. I cannot believe my eyes. I am so proud of you. I shall now return to my own part of the world a happy man. Thank you"

Outside and piled high against the back of the cabin, Uncle Asasta saw a mountain of chopped logs. And inside the cabin. The hearth was burning bright. He also saw that the young family were sitting on good solid stools around a strong table piled high with all manor of sustenance. The floor had been covered with thick rugs, and there were beds for all the family covered with many furs. Uncle Asasta was happy. This small family had now become a part of a large family. He knew now that they would never suffer again. It was now time for him to return home. However, as he departed the cabin, his friend Paddlefoot Rattail stood in his path.

"Where may I ask are you going Uncle Asasta?"

"I am returning to my home Paddlefoot. You will keep your promise and allow me to remain the man that I am?"

"Yes of course Uncle Asasta, However, I am not finished with you yet"

"Why, what more do you ask of me?"

"Much Uncle Asasta, much. Did not Frixy inform you that the proposal we wished to put before you would not only benefit the human race but yourself also?"

"Yes"

"When you look upon these villagers Uncle Asasta. Whom do you see?"

"Human beings Paddlefoot"

"I am afraid that you have been deceived Uncle Asasta. You are in fact looking upon the Elfin. They have lived in Flowsten longer than we who have lived in the forest. The village is hidden from the human race and will remain so for all time. You Uncle Asasta will now and for all time live as a member of the Elfin. Uncle Asasta, on the eve of Christmas, all children will know their fathers by the name the Elfin have bestowed upon you"

"May I ask the name that I have been blessed with?"

"Why. You are Santa Clause, of course"

A FAIRYTALE OR NOT

Look back to the oak

Sir

    My name is of no importance: however, I have a tale that I hope will verify the actual events that led up to the deaths of Robinson Black, his wife Tilly and their daughter Emily. I knew Robinson Black for a short time whilst serving on HMS Bounty, under the captaincy of William Bligh. I also knew his daughter for a short time and was fortunate enough to watch her departure from this cruel world. Parts of my tale come from what I have witnessed with my own eyes and ears; the rest comes from what I have been told by friends of the family. It is immaterial to me if you prefer not to believe my tale, for the family no longer live on this planet to suffer at the cruel whims of the scum that dictate and rule with an iron rod. In fact, the Black famly now live happily in the realms of the departed. Robinson Black owned a plot of land a mile from the town of Portsmouth. He had a cottage built on the land and lived a happy and peaceful life with his wife and daughter. He also owned a workshop in the town centre where he employed a number of men skilled in carpentry. Unfortunately, Press-gangs do not discriminate whom they force enrolment into HMS Navy. I was on board HMS Bounty when Robinson was dragged unconscious on deck with wounds to his head and was fortunate in becoming as good a friend as any. We talked much about

A Fairytale Or Not

his family and business before he gave up his ghost to the monster that respected his crew less than the ship rats. On the day that Robinson had been dragged on deck, he lay where he had been dropped for more than half a day. And when he finaly awoke, he declared

"Blimey. I feel like I've been shat on from a mile high"

From that moment, he and I were as brothers. The captain and his number one were standing forward on the bridge when the monster called out

"Stand to if you please Mr Christian"

Mr Christian had needed not bother the order because all could hear the captain's voice, not only above deck but also below. When the monsters voice was heard, not one man dares delay. And, when he had the crew cowering beneath his feet, he began his usural and unwanted speech.

"My name is William Bligh. I am the captain of the Good ship HMS Bounty on which you find yourselves. For the benefit of the men that have just joined the ship. I thank you for accepting the kings shilling and welcome you on board. You will find me to be a fair man. However, beware my wrath. If any man amoung you puts a foot in the wrong direction you will find me to be a very revengeful man. This morning, I received a report that two 25lb cheeses are missing. If the thief stands forward now, he will save his crew-mates the discomforts of hunger"

Seth Jones stood forward and attempted to explain the reason for the missings cheeses.

"Captain Sir. If you will permit me speech without the threat of punishment?"

The captain looked down upon the poor man as if he was a piece of shit he had stepped on.

"Very well man. Where are the cheeses?"

Seth looked back to the captain wishing he had kept his mouth shut. He knew the captain to be the thief as did he know the punnishment for speaking against the captain.

"Sir, whilst docked at Portsmouth harbour. You approached me with orders to take the said cheeses to the house of your mistress and that I was to inform the maid that the said cheeses were from the captain of the Bounty with his complements. Perhaps you have forgotten your orders sir?"

The colour of the captain's skin became a dark crimson and to save face he acted the part of an innocent man.

"I am the captain of this ship and say to you sir that no such order was given. You sir, are the thief but would put the guilt on your captain. Is that not the truth sir?"

It mattered not an iota as to the pleadings of Seth Jones. The captain is the law, judge and in Blighs case, the executioner. As far as that monster was concerned, the captain can do no wrongs. And although one other was present when the order was given, Seth Jones was taken below deck and put in the brig were he was to await the captains pleasure. After Seth was taken away, the captain spoke to the crew again.

"Is there any other man that would speak to his captain?"

Robinson stood forward.

"Yes. I wish to speak"

The captain was not at all happy as to Robs approach.

"When you speak to me sir, you will address me as captain"

Rob would have nothing of it and said his piece.

"I see you as an equal and no better than any man on board this ship. I am not a member of this crew but the proprietor of a well-known company in the town of Portsmouth. I have a wife and child to support. You sir, will return me to Portsmouth docks Immediately".

Once again did the captain become the colour crimson and started shouting his ugly mouth off.

"How dare you speak to me in that manor? Did you not accept the kings shilling?"

"I did not sir. Nor would have I even in hunger. I sir was press-ganged. I sir am a free man"

One of the gang members who had brought Rob on board stood forward.

"Sir. I was the man who offered this man the kings shilling. He took it with glee in his eyes. I have witnesses who saw this man put the coin into the inside pocket of his waistcoat"

The captain took great pleasure in giving the order for the gang's search of Robs clothing.

"Search the man Mr Drinkwater. By force if necessary. If there is a shilling in his pocket. He will be punished severely"

Of course, there was a shilling in Rob's pocket. He had had his wallet taken after he had been knocked unconscious only to be replaced with the coin. That scumbag known to you sir as Captain William Bligh sneered his final order of the day.

"Take that piece of dung to the brig for his insolence"

The following morning whilst doing my turn at the wheel. I watched Seth Jones climb to the crow's nest where he remained three days without rest, food or water. On the third day, the first mate asked the captain to relieve the poor man. However, the captain argued that the man in the crows nest was a thief and that as punisment; he was to remain in the nest another four days. Mr Christian raised his voice and told Bligh that the man in the nest would not survive another day let alone four days. However, the captain would not back down insisting that the thief should continue the punishment to the fullest. Mr Christian lowered his voice to a whisper, yet still did I hear every word said between them.

"Mr Bligh. You seem to have forgotten that I was present when you gave Mr Jones the order to take the cheeses that you stole, to the house of your mistress"

"That is as may be Mr Christian. However, you seem to have forgotton that we three were the only men in hearing distance. Can you prove for Mr Jones Mr Christian? I think not"

"As you say Mr Bligh, that is as may be. However, everyman on board this vessel has witnessed your sadistic punishment. I asure you Mr Bligh that your sadistic cruelty to the men on board this ship will be reported on our return to England"

"Mr Christian. Do you think that you will return to England? And, Mr Christian. If by chance, you do return to England. I will make sure that you remain on board as duty officer until the ship resets sail. Now Mr Christian. What have you to say for yourself?"

At that moment, I heard a scream. I looked up to see the fall of Seth Jones to the deck and death. Robinson was held in the brig a full week with one ladle of water a day as company. On his release, he was taken up on deck to receive the captain's favorite punishment. One dozen lashes from the cat of nine tails. However, Bligh's punishment did not deter Robinson. Refusing all and any orders Bligh gave saying that as a free man Bligh had no authority over him. Eventually, Bligh had an innocent man keelhauled. My friend did not survive the punishment. In addition. Due to the monsters idea of sport, most the officers refused to partake of the luxurious foods that Bligh ate at his pleasure. The rest of the crew had very little. And what food we did have was forced down our guts on Blighs orders even though it was maggot invested. That evil man cared not for the health of his crew even to the point of malnutrition, dysentery and death. As far as the men on board the Bounty were concerned, Bligh was the devils spore. One poor man, a Mr Mathew Savage, asked Bligh if there was any chance that he could have a little meat that did not offend the palate. The man died from the infected wounds that were inflicted upon his broken body by the cat of nine tails. Bligh seemed to get some form of sadistic sexual pleasure from the mens sufferings. The more they suffered, the more he enjoyed it. After the death of Mathew Savage, there was talk amongst the men of mutiny. However, Mr Christian promised that if we stayed loyal to the ship. Bligh would be explaining his crimes to Admiralty house. On reaching Tahiti, I jumped ship and remained hid for the months that she had been anchored just of the islands. And when at last HMS Bellerophon arrived, I approached the captain and told him that my father is an Englishman and my mother, a native of the islands. I told him that it was a wish of mine to visit the island of my father. The captain looked me up very suspiciously and sent for the list of absconding sailors. However, after reading the list for some minutes of which seemed hours to me, I was greatly relieved to hear that my name was not on the list. Although, he did say something to the effect that I am as genuine as the angel that was standing behind me. I was given permission to board the ship and work my passage to England. Now when there is a ship in harbour I will not take my drink in any public house in Portsmouth. Nor will I take to the dark lanes preferring to hide as far away from the town as possible. I will not be press-ganged again. I do not know if Bligh has yet answered for his crimes or whether he has received the punishment, he so richly deserves. However, knowing how justice is dealt on this island. I doubt very much that he has received a single reprimand but believe him to have been greatly rewarded for returning to England with his precious breadfruits. Anyhow, before my friend was murdered by that thing you call human. Robinson Black gave me explicit directions to his home and family should I ever get the chance to visit with news of their loved one. However, on the day I did visit the address given me. A nasty little man answered the door and told me in so many words to get off his property. I asked him if I had made a mistake in that I had the wrong address. I gave him the names Tilly and Emily Black. However, the imp like creature just spat and swore at me telling me to get my filthy carcass off his property. It was only by chance that I met a friend of Robinson whilst supping at the Old Hag public house. He was a little aware from too much drink and spoke aloud with bitterness in his heart. I heard him mention Robinson and Tilly many times and of his hatred for the authorities. I felt that I should introduce myself to the man and it was not long after the introduction, that we found ourselves walking some miles to his cottage well away from the town. Of course, I will not indulge in the supplying to you the identity of the man because; I believe it would be a matter of days before his arrest. I will not give you that pleasure. Therefore, when I speak of the man, I shall call him Tom. Tom and I spoke much of Robinson and his family. He told me that he was present when the letter arrived and had to witness the cruel death of little Emilys mother. He told me of the manner in which a nasty little man threw the child out of her home and how she was shown to the old hollowed oak that stands on the outskirts of Portsmouth. And of this oak, that had long ago been the residence of the little people. He told me that he still had the letter in his possession and that if I so wished, I could read it. He had not to ask me twice.

Admiralty House
14th November 1822

Mrs Tilly Black

It is with regret that I have to report the capital punishment of Robinson Black for the crime of cowardliness whilst serving on HMS Bounty.

18th February 1822. Robinson Black was hung by the neck until death. His body was buried at sea.

18th February 1822. All properties owned by the deceased are forfeit and now belong to the crown.

You and your daughter may continue to live at the property known as the Oaks for a weekly rent of 7/-

If you so wish, you may contribute a further 3/-per week toward the upkeep of the property.

Long live the king.

Sincerely Rear Admiral Lord Eima R Swipe

Tom told me that after Tilly had read the filthy, lying piece of rubbish, she fell to the floor cluching her chest with her little daughter kneeling at her side crying
"Please don't leave me mummy"
It took more than an hour before Tilly Black died in the arms of her young daughter and but a few moments later, there was a knocking at the door. It was the imp.
"Hello little girl. Is your mother home?"
The poor girl's eyes were full of tears.
"My mother's soul is winging its way to Heaven"
Not knowing that Tom was still in the property and out of sight, the caller turned very nasty. He told Emily that he was the rent collector and that the rent now due had approached £14 in arrears. He ran his filthy hands down the girls frame and told her that if she had not the capital to pay in full. There was another method of payment. Tom sprang from out of the room of the dead woman and grabbed at the throat of the man calling him a perverted little pimp. Shame he had not the strength to send the man's soul to Hell. Anyhow, Tom took Emily to his home and informed his wife as to what had transpired. And that he intended to keep the girl with them and to bring her up as their own daughter. Tom and his wife told Emily that the wicked little man would return with the baliff and forcibly have her thrown of the property only to take the place as his own. In addition, it was but a few hours later that that slimy little man was banging on the front door of Toms cottage and in tow, he had with him the local constable. Tom grabbed at the man's lapel with every intention of putting his fist to the man's nose. However, the constable stepped between the two men. The imp told to the constable in so many words to vulgar to repeat.
"Arrest this man for the kidnapping of this poor, innocent young girl. And, for attempting to cause me great bodily harm"

"I do not think so Mr Evale. What prove have you of any so-called kidnapping or come to that of any other crimes that you say this man has committed?"

"The girl is in the mans home and you yourself had reason to step between us so as to stop the man from attacking me"

"Mr Evale. I came along with you to this man's home because you are in the pay of certain authorities that I have no control over. As I understand it. This girl arrived at this man's property to ask for direction. And I most certainly did not step between you and this man to stop him from attacking you but, quite the opposite"

The imp gave the four people standing at the front door a look of utter disgust and went his way leaving the two men to discuss Emily's plight.

"I am sorry Tom. You know the type of man Mr Evale is. Now that good king George, the fourth has come into even more property, I.e. Emily's. There is very little either of us can do for her. In his eyes. Emily Black has paid no rent for his property and has no intention to do so. Therefore, Emily Black is an outcast. She cannot receive any food or any help from any persons unless authorised by the good king himself. That is something he would never give. In fact, if truth was to be heard. HRH George the 4th is no more than an unpopular, unwanted, dissipating monster. His subjects forced to hunger so as to pay extra taxes for his amusements. Although I am a constable and have sworn an allegiance to the king. He was not on the throne when I signed up. I have no respect for the man or his little goblins. Neither do I have any respect for the filthy rich that look down upon people such as us as if we are shit beneath their shoes. Had I had allowed Mr Evale to take the girl with him; he would have used her body to satisfy his perversions. I know of an old oak tree that stands a short distance from the station. It is a tree that not a soul will near, because it was long ago, the residence of the little people. I believe there is still magic there today as do I believe the little people will overcome this girl's problem"

Tom was also told that it would be best for him and his good wife to pack as much as they could take and depart from there home before Mr Evale could muster his thugs and return. Tom took his advice. Preferring to lose there home, he and his wife were gone from the place before nightfall. 10pm 21st December 1822. I met Tom. 8am 22nd December 1822. I met Emily. She was standing beneath her tree pleading for food to passers-by. Some people were kind however, fearing the authority's cruelties; they had no other choice but to leave the scene with tears in their eyes. Others were just plain evil. I heard one old woman explain to Emily.

"I am so sorry my lovely. I only wish I could help you. The authorities tax me to the point of extinction. They have told me that if I can afford to give to people whom in their eyes are criminally intent. I can afford to give to the poor old king and his parasites"

I also heard a young woman say to the child.

"I would not give to you the stench from out of my backside. Beggar"

I approached the girl calling out her name but she became afraid of me and was up the tree as a squirrel disappearing into the branches. 8am 23d December 1822. I arrived at the tree to find Emily standing at its foot shivering. She wore on her person but an old cotton frock and had nothing on her tiny feet. Her skin hung loosely on her bones and again, I saw that not one person could not or would not help her. I approached her gingerly informing her that I had known her father and that we had become as brothers whilst serving on the Bounty. I held out a parcel of food to her of which she took thanking me. However, no sooner had she opened her parcel did the evil little rent collector arrive and snached the food from out of her hand. Then looking to me, he growled

"You take me for a fool. I knew what you were up to when I saw you yesterday. Well as you like this tree so much, you will wait at its side until I return with the constable"

I held my temper but not for long

"Do you actually expect me to do as you dictate you vile little man? I intend to take this child away with me and to keep her as my daughter. If you do not like my intentions, you can eat my shit"

"I would have you know sir that I have friends in high places. You will do as I say sir or you will suffer the consequences"

I hit him hard on the nose and must admit that I thoroughly enjoyed seeing him hit the ground with a thud. I turned to face Emily to ask if she would go with me but she had disappeared up the tree and into her hollow. I picked up the parcel and threw it as high as was possible into the branches and then returned to my place of residence. 8am 24th December 1822. I arrived at the tree with another food parcel for the poor girl. She was standing at its foot with a countenance of fear expressed on her face. I had not the chance to hand her the parcel because I was pounced on from behind. It was the constable. "Mr Evale. Is this the man that knocked you to the floor yesterday?"

"Yes. That is the man. Arrest him"

"Constable, I agree that I hit the little twerp. He stole the food I had given her. Is this child to starve to death on the so say of this monster?"

The imp stood grinning as I took another swing, this time hitting him square on the mouth. The punch was enough to push him against the tree and as he did so, I would swear that I saw hundreds of tiny hands appear and pull his body through the bark. The constable grabbed at my arm

"Please sir, come with me"

He took me to the station where I was kept as a guest for the night enjoying the constables company and his good food. He explained to me, as did Tom, of Emily's predicament and of his opinions as of today's politics. He told me that because I had been at sea for so long, I knew nothing of the sufferings of the people of Great Britain since the new king had been crowned. He told me that HRH George the fourth was a greedy fool who cared not for the poor and that thanks to this king, the people of Great Britain were forced to abide to the rules of such men as the imp I had sent to the little people the day before. The time was 730am Christmas day and I wanted to get to the tree and Emily. The constable noted my pleading eyes.

"You go sir. Take the girl as your own daughter. And have a very happy Christmas"

He had need to say no more. I was up and away as the wind toward the tree and Emily. However, twenty feet from the tree, I stopped in my tracks. I saw a couple standing and facing it and relized that the man was my old friend Robinson. At his side, I knew the woman to be his wife and running toward them was their daughter Emily. She collided into their open arms, and all was as it should be. Her mother pointed to the tree.

"Look Emily. Look back to the oak"

The child did as she was asked and saw, as did I. Lying at the foot of the tree and using the snow as a blanket, a young girl called Emily. Tom and I have become as good as friends have, as was I with my departed friend Robinson. A short while ago, Tom met up with one of Robs employees. He told Tom that neither he nor any man that worked for Rob, continued their employ after the day they received information as to their new employer. Tom was also told that not one person has volunteered their services to the new owner. And, that indeed the business has collapsed and the property in ruins. I am sure that this has pleased Robinson and his family as it has very much pleased me. As for you and your kind, may you live lives in misery. So that on the day of judgement, and the hearing of the grinding of teeth. Perhaps you will understand the wickedness of your ways. And be forgiven.

A FAIRYTALE OR NOT

The forester

Friends. Please allow me to introduce myself. Fredric Albert Grant. Born to Harold and Rosemary Grant 3rd Feburary 1674 thus, making me 25 years this day. I wish to tale to you a true story about an ancestor of mine who was born more than 200 years ago. Yet, I do believe that my story has still yet to end. You I am sure will understand my reasoning after you have read this tale. I myself came about the story a few days ago whilst visiting the forest of Savernake that stands on the outskirts of the town of Marlborough in the county of Wiltshire. I wonder where to begin. If I give the story to you as it was given to me; your minds will feast well and truly enjoy the meal. However, before I begin my tale, I will say to the idiots that would have me before the authorities as a meddler in the dark arts and who would enjoy my incarceration in the tower before my agonies of the torch. They can take my tale as an entertainment and nothing else. However, imagine if you please the tale to be true. 22 January 1470 AD. Mr Samuel Grant and Miss Mary Goddard was to be wedded at 3 and 30 of the clock in the 13th century chapel that stands in the grounds of Lawns woods in the town of Swindon and in the county of Wiltshire. However, thanks to the forest fairies intervention, history was never to record the event. Samuel had lived and worked in the forest as far back when he was knee high to a grasshopper. He had very little memory of his father because he had died before Samuel had reached the age of six years. Apparently, on a quiet morning, his father had gone deep into the forest. He had been working on a giant Elm for some days and wanted to finnish the job before the weekend. Unfortunately, the man's mind was not fully on his work because he was found trapped under the trees heavy branches, lifeless. The tree had crushed his body to a pulp thus; he was not moved from the spot for fear that the body would fall apart. A priest was summonsed and burial prays were spoken before the body was covered with the soils from the forest. Immediately after the body was covered, the burial party departed the forest and returned to their homes. In those times, people believed fairy folk to be wicked little demons. Of course, these days we know differently. They are no more wicked than you nor I. Samuel lived with his mother in the cabin his father had built long before he met and married his widow. Whilst Samuel worked in the forest, his mother took in washing for the wife of the town's magistrate and although neither earned much, they found that when they pooled their pay, there was sufficient to feed not only themselves but also their friends, the wild life and the fairy folk. In fact, it could never be said that a single animal of the forest had any fear of mother nor son. In addition, the creatures fed from their hands and allowed the stroking of feather or fur without flinching. Many a night mother and son would stand outside their cabin enjoying the company of their friends and not realize that dawn was upon them until they had need to shade their eyes from the sun and heard the echoing sounds of their feathered friends as they sang their early morning songs throughout the forest. Every morning before Samuel went off to do his daily work, his mother would say

"Now Samuel, beware the fairy rings, they will take you away to an enchanted world and never allow you to return to me"

"Mother, you say the same thing to me every morning and every morning I tell you that I have been a forester all the days of my life. I know where the rings are and am always prepared for them. Never will there be the day that I shall be caught"

One day when Samuel returned home. He found that his mother was absent. He searched high and low and called out for her in the hope that even had she been injured, she may still have the strengh to answer. He went into the town of Marlborough and asked of her without success. He even walked as far as the town of Swindon only to return home disappointed. Days turned into weeks, weeks turned into months and months turned into years. He had lost his mother to the fairy folk. Swindon town stands some twelve miles from Marlborough and it was to the cattle market held in Swindon, that Samuel travelled three days a week to sell his ware, I.e. firewood, forest plants and edible fungi. It was at the cattle market that he met and fell in love with Mary the daughter of a wealthy merchant. In addition. When Samuel told Mary of his lifestyle, in that he owned and lived in a cabin that stood deep in the forest. And of how he fed from the fruits of the forest and provided himself of all that he needed by selling his wares from the forest, she accepted that her beloved had very little capital and loved him the more.

* True love can be stretched without limit. It cannot, and never be broken*

The date of the wedding was set and it was not long before Samuel was up before the dawn bird's choir and marching through his domain. He was to meet with a friend who owned a horse and trap and who was to meet Samuel at the top of the hill that led down from the forest and into the to town. As Samuel marched his way through the forest, he realised that although he had very little capital. He in fact, was a very rich man. For it mattered not the season spring, summer, autumn or winter. He had the beautiful foliage that the forest surrendered unto him; it also fed and protected him. In addition, he had his four legged friends, fox, deer, badger and many others, plus his birds. He had lived and worked in the forest all the days of his life and knew his domain well. He knew where to look for the fairy rings and was not going to be snared, as was his mother some ten years previous. Samuel Grant stepped into the centre of a fairy ring. For a brief moment, his vision had been fogged out and as the fog dispersed, Samuel realised he no longer stood upon the path that he and his friends had walked many a year. Now he stood upon a pathway unknown to him and he realized to his delight all the colours of the seasons. This was plenty prove that he was in the land of the fairies. Not one plant could he give name to that showed its beautiful face and lavished its wonderful perfume to any passerby wishing to take in its scent. Neither could he put name to a single shrub that stood heavy with delicious fruits. Nor could he claim to name one tree that stood above fifty feet and showered him with sweet nuts. He looked high above the trees and saw that although the warm sun was in its zenith, there was no glare. The intake of air that he enjoyed was good and clean, and there was a slight breeze filtering through the trees that stood on either side of him. The lush green grass that his feet stood upon led to a magnificent castle in the far distance. He could see that the structure was of the purest white and contained many windows, far too many for the count. Beyond the castle, Samuel saw mountains reaching up through the clouds and Heavenward. And running down the sides of the mountains were torrents of pure water. He also saw that the castle stood in many hundreds of acres of lush green fields boasting beautiful blue lakes and rivers. And surrounding all this magnificence was a beautiful forest. Samuel wanted to be at the castle before nightfull so that he could seek the help of the fairies to return him home and to his beloved Mary. However, after a considerable lengh of time had elapsed, Samuel began to think that he was not to reach his objective. And before long, he was tormented by thirst and hunger and wished for the waters from the mountains so far away.

"If you so wish sir, you may quench your thirst from the river that runs at your side. After you have quenched your thirst sir, I must ask you to follow me"

"What the. Who said that?"

"I am called Frogtooth sir. I am standing but two feet before you"

"Why can I not see you?"

"You cannot see me sir because you have not had audience"

"I do not understand. What is audience?"

"Their royal majesties sir. You have not had audience. When you have had audience sir, you will be able to see me"

"How am I to follow you Frogtooth when it is quite clear that you are invisible to me?"

"The foot prints sir, see the foot prints"

Samuel looked down to the ground and sure enough, he saw the footprints of a tiny person form in the centre of the pathway that led to the distant castle. He had quite forgotten his thirst and remembering Frogtooth's first words to him. He looked down to his side and saw the river. The waters were as clear as is glass and Samuel also saw the beautiful creatures that lived beneath its surface. He took in great gulps of pure sweet water and as did his thirst disperse, so did his hunger.

"Has your thirst been satisfied sir?"

"Yes thank you Frogtooth. Please leed on"

"The footprints sir, follow the footprints"

Samuel watched in astonishment as each tiny foot left its print in the ground as they sped off as the wind. And as his feet fell close to the heels of his guide, Samuel called out

"Does the sun never set in this world of yours Frogtooth?"

"Oh yes sir, when it is required"

"When is it required Frogtooth?"

"When we take to our sleep sir, then do the creatures of the night become active"

"How do the creatures of the night differ from you, Frogtooth?"

"You will see for yourself sir, after you have had audience"

At every footfall, the distant structure became larger until; finally, they arrived at the steps leeding up to the towering entrance doors. Samuel looked up to the magnificent sight. Such splendour he could never describe. Of course, he had heard of and even visited some of the castles where the rich folk lived. In adddition, he had heard of the magnificent palace that stood in the capital of Great Britain and its occupants, the royal family. However, in comparison with the structure he now stood before, the palace of the royal family were but mud huts.

"If you please sir, follow the sound of my voice"

Samuel followed the voice of his companion up a hundred pure white marble steps and up to two massive solid oak doors that had been studded with every gemstone imaginable. Each door had its own golden hand ring pull. And each door had been swung open to its fullest to reveal a great hallway of many doors on either side. The walls were adorned with tapestries containing such splendid scenes that Samuel had to wonder if they were actual or from the mind of the artist. Every door along the full lengh of the hallway had been fashioned from the same wood as was the entrance doors. And, carved on every door was a single creature such as the majestic Unicorn, the ever-knowing Centaur. There was the mighty Griffin and the bird born from the ashes of fire, the Phoenix. The half man half bull Minotaur. Water Nymph and even a nasty little Imp. Not one door contained the same image and yet there were hundreds. Will-o-the-wisp, Goblin, Troll, Elf, Fairy, Warlock, Witch. Name any creature that comes to mind, its image had been carved onto one of the many hundreds of doors. Marble flooring lay beneath his feet, and when he looked up to wonder at the marvels of the decorated ceiling, he saw a beautiful clear night with many shining silver stars and a beaming full moon. And whilst Samuel took in all this splendour, to his delight, he watched the magnificent Pegasus fly over the palace and out of sight. Samuel was led up and down many flights of stairs and along many hallways of which were as splendid as was the first until finally he was led into a room of no end. Although Samuel could hear much chattering, still could he not see the creatures that made sound. Also, whilst Samuel had been following his guide up and down the many flight of stairs and along the many hallways, his eyes had fed upon many delights. However, this final room he had been led into was unbelievable. How could such splendour exist? Yet hear was the proof of it. The flooring was that of dark oak with the shine of clear glass. Standing upon the flooring were a hundred tables of the same material and of the same shine. Each table measured four feet across and travelled the full lengh of the room without end. In fact, Samuel could see his reflection on the floor and on the surface of the tables as if he was looking at himself in a mirror. In addition, on every side of every table stood benches of the same quality. Every table had been adorned with beautiful place settings. Goblets of crystal that had been impregnated with pure gold. Serving platters made from precious metals, and encrusted with gemstones. Cutlery and utensils made from the purest of silver also encrusted with precious and beautiful gemstones. And when Samuel looked to see the walls and how they had been decorated, he saw not a single wall but lush green lawns surrounded by the beautiful forest ablaze with lanterns hung about the tress. And, dancing and playing among the trees, Samuel saw many of the mystical creatures that he had seen carved upon the many doors that his escort Frogtooth had led him by.

"If you please sir, follow the sound of my voice"

On and forward did Samuel and his guide, until they arrived in the front of two solid gold thrones.

"If you please sir, remain where you stand until you hear voices other than mine speak your name"

A familiar voice called out Samuels name and from that moment, he saw as far as his eyes would permit the creatures that had made chattering on his arrival in the room. Sitting on the benches, he saw all kind of fairy folk. Brownies, Elves, Nymphs, Leprechauns, Phoukas, Ganconers and many others, far too many to tell. He returned his gaze to the thrones and saw sitting on them, his parents. They looked to be twice as young as he was. On their heads, they wore crowns of gold. And, attached to their backs, they bore the wings of angels. Tears of joy ran down all three faces and they all three hugged one another for such a time that it seemed never to end. At last, Samuels's mother broke loose and spoke to her son. "Samuel. We are a fortunate people because there are those amoung us that see the future. Many years before you were born, these people came to us with warning of terrible happenings in the world of the human beings. In the twentieth and twenty-first centuries, demons, will be loosed upon their world. Outside, these monsters will look to be human. However, inside, only evil will exist. There will be many thousands of these demons, and all will be loyal to their master. When the sign of the swastika is worn, many millions of innocents will die. Many years will pass and still will there be demons whose names will be remembered in futures history. Adolf Hitler, Idi Amin, Saddam Hussein, Robert Mugabe, Kim Jong-il, King Muammar Al-Qaddfi, Fidel Castro, Hu Jintao, Seyed Ali Khamenei, Omar Al Bashir, Islam Karimov, Saparmurat Niyazov are but a few of these evil creatures. There will be corrupt governments, and there will be greedy businessmen. There will be thiefs and thugs of all kind and of all ages. And whilst the weak and the innocent suffer and are punished for defending themselves, their loved ones and their properties, laws will be made to protect the guilty. Samuel, when you were born to us. It was felt, that you should live in the world of the humans for a reason. You have now lived thirty years in their world and know them for what they are. Times will come when they will have need of our assistance. We will forever be there for the hot at heart, but as for the cold at heart, they will not know us. Do not fear the future my son for you are a prince of the sprite, and forever shall you have command of a great sprite army. When wars are arrived and an innocent is taken. You will be there to hold back Hells demon carriers from delivering the souls of the innocent to their master. You will know truth from lies. You will know love from hatred and you will know good from evil"

"Mother, you have told me that I will know good from evil. Will you please give me an example?"

"Yes my son. The wicked shall have streaks of yellow running down the full lengh of their vile spines and they shall spit from out of their mouths brown waste. You shall see them as murdering dictators, thugs, vandals, perverts, self-praising morons, thieves, and malingerers. The eyes of a human being are the windows to their souls. A human being with a good soul shall be unblemished. A human being with a wicked soul shall be blemished. An unblemished soul you will assist, a blemished soul you will not assist. Samuel my son. This is your destiny. Because you are a sprite. Because you have the magic of the fairies. Because you are a prince of the fairies"

"Mother I understand all that you have told me and accept this as my destiny. However, this morning, I was to meet and marry my Mary in the old chaple in Swindon. Although it is very late now, please allow me to return to her world so as to bring her back here where we can be married in this our land" Samuels's parents looked to their son with pity showing in their eyes and then his father spoke.

"My son, you cannot return to your Mary because she no longer exists in the realm of the living. Her soul now resides with her ancestors as a free spirit in another"

Samuel refused to hear these words and inssited that he be returned to the world he had lived all the days of his life. His parents and that of his kindred, desperately but in vain pleaded with Samuel to stay in the world of the sprite. However, he refused to believe or listen.

"Samuel, if you return to the world of the human beings, it could be many hundreds if not thousands of years before you return to this world"

But it was not until his parents agreed to their sons demand that they enjoyed the rest of the evening together after which with much sadness, Samuel was escorted by many sprite to the very chapel the prince was to wed his Mary. They arrived early morning and after saying his farewells to his new friends, Samuel prowled the grounds until such time that the priest should arrive. In addition, Samuel noted that in the short time he had been in the realm of his parents, the yard had quadrupled in the number of graves. He wandered the yard until nine of the clock when he heard the old iron gates creak open on their hinges and saw an old woman enter. She was wearing a long black dress and had the hood of the dress up above her head. As she came near enough for him to see her face, he became dumb struck and held a look of disgust on his face. The woman was in fact a man.

"Can I be of assistance to you my son?"

"How dare you call me your son? You have no right in the entering of these holy grounds. You are abomination"

"I am father Joseph Mc'Pheason my son"

"Bull shit! My father wears not the clothing of a woman. You are a homosexual"

"Ah, now I understand your reasoning my son. The garment that you see me wearing is not the garment of a woman. It is called a Smock. It is the cloth of a priest my son"

"Will you please stop calling me your son? My father lives err! A long way from here"

"Very good. I will stop calling you my son. May I ask what business you have in the chapel my boy?" "Err, I am not sure?"

"Perhaps if you start from the beginning my boy?"

"Yesterday, I was to be wedded to my Mary. However, I cannot give reason for my lateness"

"My boy, you have most certainly got your dates mixed up. There has not been a wedding in this chapel for over fifty years. Actually, this is the reason for my presence here this morning. There is to be a wedding ceremonial at noon. By special permission of course. I am here to prepare the chapel for the blessed marriage of the right honourable Sir Alfred Charles and the Lady Joanna Patterson"

"I have not heard of them nor do I have any interest in them what so ever. My name is Samuel Grant and I was to be wedded to Mary Goddard yesterday"

"I am afraid that you are mistaken my boy. Have I not just a moment ago told you that there has not been a wedding here for more than fifty years?"

"How could I have made such a mistake? Do you truly think me a dolt? I asure you that I have my faculties about me. And, I do know what the date is"

"What date do you believe it to be my boy?"

"It is the 22nd day of January 1470 of course"

The priest stood and thought for a while before asking Samuel to wait for his return. He entered the chapel and returned shortly after with a large book covered in a thick dust.

"Just as I suspected my boy. There are remarks regarding a wedding that should have taken place on the date you have specified. However, for an unknown reason, it was cancelled because Samuel Grant did not arrive for the ceremony. There are also remarks regarding Mary Goddard. She lived until the great age of ninety-three. She died a spinster. And as for Samuel Grant. He disappeared from the face of the planet. The records say that the fairy folk took him. And may I say. Who are we to argue for apparently that same Samuel Grant is standing before me this day"

"Yes it is true. I have been with the fairies. However, I have only been away for a matter of twenty-four hours. Please tell me. In what year do I now stand?"

"My boy, you have returned to the year 1674"

In the twenty-four hours, Samuel had spent with his parents. Two hundred years had flown past in the world that you and I live. Of course, Samuel did marry. Had he not; I would not be here to tell this story. Last Saturday whilst visiting the forest of Savernake. I met a man of who persisted in the keeping of his eyes to the ground. I asked him if he had lost anything of importance. He told me that he had not but that he was serching for a fairy ring. He then told me a story. That story, I have now passed onto you.

A FAIRYTALE OR NOT

Doorway to Paradise perhaps!

If there are people living on this planet one thousand years from now. I pray that this parchment will fall into the hands of those that it is intended. My name is Blyth Sawyer and I intend that this testament shall shock you into seeking the help of those that will have in their possession for their safekeeping and your protection this document. I am a married woman living in the year 0999 AD and now find myself standing and waiting my turn to enter through the doorway on this first millennium. I can only hope and pray that the moment I pass over the threshold, there will be waiting in the new world, my husband and children. However, before I leave this our world forever. I shall hand this parchment to the little people. They will know when the time has arrived to re-enter this world and assist the deserving. Long before I was born to this world, even perhaps before the measurment of time. The land was a mass of forest. In addition, living in the waters that surround the land, there are hideous creatures. One of these creatures, we call the Kraken. If a man looked into the eyes of this creature, he will become stone. There are monsters in the waters with many arms. Each arm has many suctions powerful enough to lift a horse. The monster also has an eye the size of a cartwheel and a beak that would crush the bones of any man that would dare enter the waters. There are fish the size of small islands, and snakes the lengh of ten men.

Yet still at this time would I prefer to live in the waters than on the land, because there is a monster ten-fold worse that has been loosed on this world. Moreover, he will be loosed again one thousand years from now. The monster has many names but we know him as Beelzebub. Beelzebub had lived in the realm of holiness with other angels, and was happy to stand in the light of the living God Jehovah. However, Beelzebub became unhappy with his lot and became as evil as evil can be. Therefore, God sent Beelezbub to a place away from Heaven for all eternity. This place, we call Hell. In Hell, Beelzebub found his disciples known to us as Demons. They are the Goblins that live deep beneath the trodden earth, the forever deluding Will-o-the-wisp, the devilish Imps that willingly slave all the days of their lives for their evil master, and the Trolls that would bite the head of any man daring to cross its path. All this happened long before the son of our living god gave up his life so that the sins of men will be washed away. And to this day, we give thanks. However, as I have told you, Beelzebub has been allowed to enter the world of Gods children and with him, he has brought along his disciples. The reason for this is that our God would know our faith. I will try to explain this statement. We have and hold dear to our hearts a book. It is written in this book that once every one thousand years; Beelzebub will be freed to roam our world with his disciples for a short time period to tempt as many people as possible with earthly possessions. If we are strong enough and we can tell him to leave us alone and take up not his offers, our souls will be redeemed as fit, and they will then be admitted entrance into the kingdom of our God whence our bodies are to tired to continue. However, if we are greedy and take up the offers of the monster, then our souls will not be redeemed as fit and we will not be permitted entrance into the kingdom of our God. Beelzebub is permitted to tempt even upon pain. However, he is not permitted the destruction of our flesh. For example, He may say to a man

"If you bow before me, I make promise that no harm will befall you. However, should you prefer to worship Jehovah. I will break every bone in your body"

If the man is a coward and will fall to his knees to the monster, he will then be lost. But, if the man is strong and will tell the fiend to depart, he will be given the strength to suffer all that Beelzebub gives, and Jehovah will send the devil away, and the man will live out his life in peace, and when his body is to tired to continue his soul will be freed from within it and welcomed entry into the kingdom of Heaven. Beelzebub is the suprem master of evil and he has not honoured Jehovah's command. He will not break the bones of a man; he will rip out the bones of a man. He will foul the food on a man's table and then sit back to enjoy the sufferings of the family as they starve to their deaths. He will poison the water in the wells and laugh when the tongues of many swell until thay can take in no breath. When first he sent out his demons with their temptations, we fought and sent them crying to their master that we would rather die than live in his evil shadow. Now the time has come that he and his followers have very little time left in our world. Soon they must return to their own realm until yet another thousand years have past. Beelzebub has sent out his Will-o-the-wisp and the wind has taken up the evil seed to disperse all over the land. Subsequently, we have now found ourselves covered from head to foot with black boils the size of horse chestnuts. After a short time, these boils burst, leaving oozing pus to enter our nostrils and mouths, thus causing many of us horrific deaths. Yet; still will we not bow our heads to him, preferring to take our chances with the creatures in the waters that lap our land. Fortunately, there is an opposite of all things. Beelzebub is evil, Jehovah is holy. There are as many good spirits on the land and in the waters as are there wicked and therefore when the wicked strike, the good come to our assistance. We call the good spirits, the little people because that is what they are, Also and thankfully, the good spirits have the same if not more magic powers as do the demons that attack us daily and are not the cowards as are the devils disciples. Therefore, when the little people use their powers on the demons, the vile things return in flight to their evil master. The little people whom stay on the land, have wings of many shapes, sizes and colours attached to their backs, and those that prefer the waters, have fins of many shapes, sizes and colours. It is common knowledge that the little people not only befriended most the mighty beasts including the magnificent unicorns that roam our world but that the beasts have accepted the little people as their masters. It is also common knowledge that these beasts will never show themselves to us unless by command of the little people. A few days ago, we were told to go to a place of which will remain a secret for the time being, where we shall be safe from the evil spirits until such time that we will take our place before the doorway and then to enter through to a dimension befitting our lives on this planet. For example, a malingering hypophondriac will find himself in a realm where the pretender will have to work for his living. Alternatively, a gluttonous man will find himself in a realm where food that keeps him alive on this planet will not be a required substance in the world that has accepted him. In the last few days that we have been here in our hiding place, we have witnessed the sufferings of six beautiful unicorns. They have each, willingly given their lives so that we can go through the door. Each of them has allowed themselves to be tethered to a pole beside a small well. A blunted blade was then put to their throats until their blood ran freely into the well. Not one unicorn attempted for escape but stood firm until their lives blood had drained. Their carcasses were then thrown unceremoniously upon red coals and left there until their ashes became cold. The ashes were then collected up and half of them were fashioned into a beautiful archway. The remaining ashes were fashioned into a door that when fixed into the archway, fitted perfectly. The whole was then painted with the blood collected from the wells. In addition, as the little people toiled, we heard them chanting their spells none stop until they had finished their work. And whilst the little people had been working, the door was kept open and when the painting had been completed; the last of the blood was spilled onto and over the threshold and finaly thrown into the unseen. The doorway was then closed and has remained so until this day 31st December 0999. This morning the door was opened and many hundreds of people have gone through it. My family entered through the doorway early this morning, had they not, they would have surly died from the Black Death. I also have the Black Death upon me and now wait my turn in the short queue before I also go through the doorway. It is regretful that many people refuse to enter through the doorway because they fear the unknown. Myself, I fear for their souls and pray for them. It is now my turn to go through the doorway but, before I leave this world. Take head my friends from the future and look to the little people. I now go through the doorway to Paradise perhaps!

A FAIRYTALE OR NOT

Visitor

8th February 1855. In the period of one night, the river Exe was frozen. Thus, leaving birds and other creatures trapped and frozen in the ice. History informs us that the winter of 1854/55 was the coldest in living memory. 9th February 1855, the snow had fallen on the county of Devon, leaving a thick blanket where an ornithologist or zoologist, would have had a field day exploring and discovering the tracks of their chosen subjects. However, there had been tracks left by a creature that our historian relatives could not identify. In fact, the people of Devon concluded that the Devil had left the tracks. In the next few pages, I will give you two counts of the same story. It of course is up to you to decide of which the true is. I prefer to believe the story told to me by an old gypsy of whom I befriended when I was no taller than the footstool that stands under my stairwell.

First count

The tracks zigzagged across over a hundred miles of land. They were found in the gardens of many homes and up to the front doors. The tracks went over rooftops and haystacks. The creature had gone into barns and even up the side of high walls. Each print measured 4 inches by 2.¾ inches and 8 inches apart. The tracks appeared to have belonged to a creature standing on two legs that boasted cloven hooves. Over the period of one night, the mysterious creature had crossed over five parishes starting at Totnes and ending in Littleham. In one village, the tracks led into a shed and through a six-inch diameter hole at the back. In another village, the tracks led up to a drainpipe, emerging at its end. Hundreds of letters reporting the phenomenom pored into the county newspapers. One of the letters received from the town of Dawlish explained that the tracks led up to and in dense undergrowth. The letter stated that many of the men folk had sent their dogs into the undergrowth to flush out the creature and that after a short time, the dogs returned to their masters howling and very much distressed. Many people tried to explain the phenomenon. One given by the knowledgable Sir Richard Owen was that a badger had left the tracks. Others suggested that they were the track of a cat, a fox, a crane or perhaps an escaped kangaroo from a circus. One man asked that due to the fact the tracks belonged to a cloven hooved creature, could it have been a horse. More suggestions arrived at the county newspapers. Could it have been a toad? Maybe a rabbit or squirrel had left the prints. Even the local vicar had to put his oar in. he told his parishioners that the traks left in the snow had been made by feral cats. The people of Devon will not be persuaded other than the Devil walked their county on the 9th day of February 1855.

Second count

Before God destroyed the cities of Sodom and Gomorrah because they were full of depravity and promiscuousness. He sent two angels to the house of Lot to give warning as to his intention. The angels told Lot to take his family out of the city of Sodom and that they were not to look back to see Gods wrath on the cities. Whilst the two angels were residing in the house of Lot there was a knocking at the door. It was abomination determing to know the angels rather than Lots daughters. (Holy Bible, Leviticus 20 verse 13. If a man lie with mankind, as he lieth with a woman, both of them have commited an abomination: they shall surly be put to death; their blood shall be upon them. However, when Lot and his family left the city, his wife could hold her curiosity no longer. She looked back to the cities and became a pillar of salt. Thus is the wrath of God. All things that God forbade and all things that are against Gods

A Fairytale Or Not

will, were performed every minute of every day throughout the whole of this world. Homosexuality, Bestiality, Rape, Adultery, Thuggery and theft were all part of everyday life until God would tolerate it no longer. He gave Noah instructions for the building of an Ark. When Noah had completed the task, God told him to take on board his wife, daughters and their husbands and to include one male and one female of every creature on this world. He was then to board the Ark himself and lock it up so that none other could enter. Noah and his family then settled down to a life of animal husbandry for many weeks. God then let open the heavens thus causing the land to be flooded and all life on it to be destroyed. At the ending of five weeks and five days, God stopped the rains and the land became dry. When the Ark landed on solid ground, Noah opened up the Ark and let free all that was on board. God then told Noah that he would never flood the land again confirming his promise with a rainbow and telling Noah that from hence forth, At the ending of a storm, so shall there appear a rainbow in rememberance of my promise. However, the seven deadly sins were soon to show their ugly heads again. Scum such as Hellogabalus the horrible, Napolean and Hitler, to name but a few of the many that have been and are yet to come. Therefore, God gave a warning that the day of judgement will see the gnashing of teeth. God put upon this planet many species of life, most of which are known to us. However, there are creatures that exist on this planet that many of us refuse to believe in. many people have heard these creatures going about their business and many people have seen them. Yet still they refuse to accept what their eyes have told them. Be assured, these creatures do exist, from the tiniest Fairy to the tallest Giant. From the Unicorn to the Centaur and from the Imp to the Goblin, they do exist. The Holy Bible does not tell us when the end of the world will come. However, when this question came about, we was told that the end of the world will be upon us when corrupt government's punish the innocent and reward the guilty. The end of the world will be upon us when corrupt governments legalise abomination *Sodom and Gomorrah* The end of the world will be upon us when corrupt governments legalise evil to walk free amoung the innocent *Nazis* The end of the world will be upon us on the changing of the seasons. All people are born equal and with a spirit. And all people have a will of their own and the knowledge of good and evil. If people choose the side of evil, then they alone will have themselves to blame when on the day of true judgement, their souls will enter into the fires of

Hell without any pity. However, most people choose the side of goodliness and to these people, God says that in his house there are many mansions and that there is a place for them in the kingdom of Heaven. The prince of darkness knows that in the father's house there will never be a place for him or any of his followers. Beelzebud wishes not to remain in Hell with just his demons for company for the rest of eternity. The devil needs to take with him as many innocents as possible so that he and his demons such as Hitler can enjoy the torturing of these souls forever. No sane man will give his soul to the devil knowing what sufferings the monster would have upon him. The winter of 1854/55 was the coldest in living memory and although the wealthy lived lives of luxury, the poor suffered from coldness and hunger. The state benefit did not exist as it does today. There were the workhouses of course but most people would rather die than enter these establishments. In addition, the people of the day could not enter into the Labour Exchange as they do today in the hope of finding employment and perhaps a few Pennies to survive on until the following week when they would re enter the establishment for yet another chance of employment and again receive a few Pennies. If there was no work, they went without. At most, the rich folk had very little time for them. These paupers of men had to watch their wifes and children go to their beds in hunger. They had to watch their families shiver in their thin clothing, and watch their children place shoeless feet into the freezing snow. Therefore, at this time when the need for comfort was most felt, the Devil sent out his Goblins with temptations. The demons visited the homes of those that suffered most with offers of food and plenty. Warm clothing for the whole family and great wealth was offered so that a family should never suffer again. And when a man asked how the debt should be paid. He was told that on the day of his death, he must give up his soul to the Devil. The Goblins travelled more than one hundred miles over the Devonshire landscape visiting all men and their families that hungered for food and warmth. From Totnes to Littleham they went. Homes, barns, rooftops, waterways, sheds and walls, and, when a man gave into temptation, the Goblin took up residence at the side of the man's soul. It would remain there until the man gave up his life and then the Goblin would carry the man's soul to its master. However, a man that would give up his soul so that his family should not suffer is not evil and he had only to ask of Gods help. *Blessed is he that asks for he shall receive* A beast was sent over the land. A beast that has not been seen on this planet and no doubt will not be seen unless you truly believe. The beast had only to touch a man that held more than one spirit in his body with the tip of its horn. Then, the wicked Goblin would be thrown from out of the man and back to its evil master, empty handed. The men were then free to enjoy their lives with their families with the knowledge that on their deathbeds, their souls would be safe in the arms of the lord.

On the 9th February 1855. 'Twas the tracks of a Unicorn that the people of Devon found in the snow.

A FAIRYTALE OR NOT

Mound

When first Mr and Mrs Underhill registered their names at the local council offices for a home, they were told that they had a choice of either a two or three-bedroom property. They were also given a choice of where they wished to live, rural or town. The Underhill's decided that they preferred rural because they had lived most of their lives in the countryside and had no desire for town life. Therefore, the Council agreed that the couple with their three daughters and two dogs would be offered a rural property. However, a few weeks later, the council decided to put the family not only into a town house but also onto an estate from Hell. I state this fact because although the estate was massive, very few decent people actualy lived on it. Most the inhabitants were very undesirable indeed. Moreover, I have recently come to know that due to the estate being widely known as the estate from hell, it was completely demolished some years ago by the Council. What happened to the slime that oozed from out of it? I have no idea, nor do I care. I only know that since the Underhills were offered a place elsewhere, they are extremely happy. When first the Underhills moved onto the estate, they had no idea that there were more undesirables than decent people. In fact, the very day they entered their home of which they stayed less than thee months. They had a knock at the front door. It was one of the very few decent neighbours. The neighbour asked the

A Fairytale Or Not

Underhills what on earth had made them move onto the estate. The Underhills explained that the move was not of their choosing but that of the council. The neighbour told the Underhills that unless they were thugs themselves or that they cowered down to the ruels of the estate thugs, they would truly be made to suffer. The Underhills asked their neighbour

"If the estate is as bad as you say, why do not the police get involved?"

The neighbour replied

"For two reasons. Firstly, they are afraid to enter the estate, and secondly, there are those on the estate that are police informers".

Therefore, the Underhills tried to settle down in their new home keeping themselves to themselves. However, because they would not bow down to the scumbag neighbours, the slime made their lives as miserable as possible. The Underhills and other decent neighbours had to put up with yobs as young as seven years of age walking along the side of their cars holding in their vile claws screwdrivers for cutting deep indentations in the paintwork. The yobs would then walk off laughing, because they knew that if their victims were brave enough to complain to the parents of the monsters, the poor victim would be warned off with threats of violence. In addition, when the same slime buckets urinated through letterbox's, the police would inform the victims that unless they had proof of the incidents, there was nothing thay could do. When one victim of the thugs informed the police that they actually stood and watched the yob urinating through their letterbox, the police even had an excuse for this

"If we get involved, you will have even more problems with other neighbours. I.e. The Mead family and their associates. It would be best for you that we stayed out of your dispute"

There was the Ness woman and her brood of little demons. These turds stole into gardens and sheds stealing all they could get their filthy claws on, destroying all that they could not and even leaving faeces on plant beds and vegetable gardens. Not satisfied with this, they then kicked footballs hard against front windows and then waited for their victims to complain to the brat's parents knowing that the victims would be threatened with violence. Even then, these monsters had to make more problems for their victims by walking up to a property and putting their ugly faces up against the window so as to look into the home. In fact, most people had their curtains closed not only at night but also through the day. The Underhill daughters were put through hell in, and away from school to a point when one actualy lost her hair through fear of the scum. The police were a waste of space only entering the estate when their drug-addicted informants invited them. Mr Underhill frequently made telephone calls to the council pleading with them to move his family away from the estate giving his reasons. However, the idiot on the other end of the line told him

"Mr Underhill, I do not believe that the problem is anywhere near as bad as you say"

Yet, this idiot knew that the estate housed ex-convicts of rape, murder, animal torture and all sorts of evil doings. It was not until Mr Underhill had made many telephone calls to the council that they eventualy sent an officer to the family home. However, when the officer arrived, he told the Underhills that the problem was not as bad as the Underhills had said, and that there was nothing he could do for them. When the moron left the Underhills to suffer the consequence's of his visit, he found that the Ness woman's yobs had shovelled wet sand through his open sunroof. He did not bother to clear it out preferring to move his arse off the estate as quick as a fart and never to return. Weeks passed by and still the estate scumbags made life difficult for the family. More telephone calls were made to the council and more excuses were made to the Underhills until once again they sent another officer to the family home.

"Mr and Mrs Underhill. As far as I understand it, Mr Stew Pide has accepted the sand incedent as a practical joke and feels that you have nothing to complaine about. If I were you, I would stop complaning about every little incedent and get on with your lives. Good day to you"

However, when she arrived at her car, she found the Mead and Ness yobs climbing onto the boot, running along the roof and sliding down the front window. I wonder if she took that as a practical joke? More weeks passed by and the Underhills heard nothing from the council. They prayed daily for heavy rainstorms so as to keep the yobs at bay. Nasty items to vulgar to mention were put through the letterbox and left on the front lawn. The children were continusly being bullied by the Mead mob and the Ness's yet still the police nor, would the council do anything for the family. Fortunately, Mr Underhill was a strong believer in the fairy folk and often left messages around the house asking of their help in getting him and his family back to his beloved countryside. And it was because of his strong believe that a few weeks after the last visit from the council that the mysterious letter arrived. It was addressed to Mr P B and Mrs J E

Underhill. And on the back of the envelope were the names of the senders, Razwigam Crode and Screir. Mr Underhill opened the envelope and read the contents.

Dear Mr and Mrs Underhill. We have the greatest of pleasure in informing you that a property has become vacant. It is five miles from the nearest village and ten miles from the nearest town. It stands inside its own grounds of two hundred acres including woodlands and fully stocked lakes. If you are interested and wish to view the property, my partners and I will be very pleased if you would call into our office Cuydownmushrooms at your earliest convenience. You will find us in Wood-green lane, Brentwood, Essex. Faithfully Your servant Fline Razwigan.

The Underhills had never heard of Fline Razwigan, Crode and Screir. In addition, although the Underhills knew Brentwood like the back of their hands, they had never seen the office of Cuydownmushrooms. It also sounded odd to the Underhills that a mushroom supplier was also renting out properties. It was also very strange that although the Underhills had very little capital and had neither heard of or approached this company for the purpose of renting a property, that the company had in fact contacted them. This was all very intriguing. It was therefore agreed by the family that although Essex was many miles from Wiltshire, they would visit the office of Razwigam, Crode and Scrier the next day. The family with their two dogs were up and off the estate at 05am praying, that they should never have to return, not even to collect their belongings, preferring the council to clear the property and sending a bill. I can tell you now that they were off that estate for good, and that although the property was empty until the estate was demolished some years later. The Underhills did not receive any bills from the council for rents or anything else. At 830am, the Underhills arrived in the small car park belonging to the company of Cuydowmushrooms. The office itself was very small and would only allow Mr and Mrs Underhill entrance so, the girls had to remain in the car whilst their parents visited their new to be landlords. The office contained one large desk that took up most of its room, and, sitting behind the desk was three little bearded men with such smiles printed on their faces that the Underhills had no need to be asked to sit. The three little men stood up and bowed to the couple and then the man with the longest beard began to talk.

"My dear Peter and June. My word, you are pretty my dear. Well, here we are after all this time. And may I say that we three all are so very privileged and honoured to be the first in greeting you. Please do not ask any questions at this time. It is enough that our kind realises that you are rightfully amoung us and that the prophesy we have waited for oh so long, has finally come full circle. We three realize that it is very difficult for you to understand our joy. However, please let me explain that Mr Crode, Mr Scrier and I are from a place that we hope very much to ask of you, your three pretty girls and of course, your beautiful dogs to enter someday in the very near future. In the meantime, we asure you that the information we sent to you, is correct. Well, perhaps we deceived you just a little. In fact, we have the greatest pleasure in informing you that you are the soul owners of the property and all that it intakes. Am I correct in saying Peter that you are a true believer in; shall we say the little people? Well, the little people have come to your rescue. Peter, you have an ancestor who owned the property more than five hundred years ago. Even then, did she know your name and that one day five hundred years in the future, you and your family would be in need of her help. Therefore, before she went her own way, she decided to put the property in the care of the little people until such time that you should come on the scene, so to speak. Now that we have you with us. We think it is time for us to show you your new home"

Before either Peter or June could say a single word, the three little men were out of the office and sitting inside the back of the car with the three girls and two dogs. Yet, there was room a plenty for all.

"I did not even see them leave the office, did you June?"

"No, very strange"

Peter and June got into the front of the car where then Mr Razwigam gave instructions in directing them to their new home.

"Turn left out of the car park Peter and follow the road for as long as it takes you. Now turn left here Peter and then left into that car park"

"Mr Razwigam. We have just done a compleat circle of your office"

"Have we really Peter? Take another look"

The family car and its occupants were parked at the side of a beautiful little country cottage surrounded by many beautiful trees and shrubs in fact the colours of the foliage had as many colours of the rainbow, and more. Their neighbours were the wild animals that also lived on the land. In addition, living with these neighbours, would be an absolute pleasure for the Underhills. The family stood and listened for the noice of traffic. There was none. They listened for the sounds of other human beings.

There was none. They would never have to listen to these sounds again. Moreover, the family were very pleased to hear the voices of the wild creatures that prowled the grounds of their new home. They listened to the sounds of the slow running waters of the nearby river that they were happy to see on their land. They listened to the noice of the leaves on the trees rustling as a soft breeze travelled its way through the branches and on to the Underhills so as to caress their warm faces in the heat of the day. Mr Razwigam looked up to Mr Underhill and spoke

"Peter, you and your family are standing on land that has never been touched by any other than those entitled. You are guaranteed unwelcome visitors will never bother you and your family again. Nor will you have need for visiting either village or town for body cloth or sustenance as these will be supplied on a daily basis. Soon you will know the meaning of my words. Until then, no more will be told you" Mr Razwigam then handed Peter a gold locket and chain and told him that the items must be kept on his person at all times even, when retiring to his bed. He told Peter

"Without this locket and chain Peter, you will not be permitted entry into our world. It is now time for us to leave you and your family. We look forward to seeing you again in the very near future"

Peter and his family turned to face the cottage and started the walk up to the front door. However, Peter remembered that Mr Razwigam had not given him any door keys. He turned back to call Mr Razwigam but there was no sight of the three little men. He turned back to face the cottage and saw that Mrs Underhill was standing at the front door holding a small parchment.

"It is a short note from Mr Razwigam, Peter. It says that there is no need for locks on these premises and that only the entitled can enter"

The Underhills entered the property and once the door was closed behind them, they all received elation so powerful that not one could hide their emotions. It was as if the magic of Christmas was upon them. Yet, it was a different kind of magic and they were soon to find out the truth. Many weeks passed by and the family had settled into their new lives when one day whilst chasing one another through the woodlands, they came upon a clearing with a circumference of fourty yards. In its centre was a mound eight feet in height, fifteen feet across and thirty feet in length. On the top of the mound, stood a beautiful tree, that none could recognize. The circumference of the trunk covered the fullness of its home and stood twice the height of any tree in the wood. In addition, its branches reached out far across the clearing, touching the lush green grass at the foot of the mound. Its fruits ready for harness, the family tasted every varity it produced. Never had they tasted such in all the days of their lives. As they enjoyed the beauty of the tree and ate of its delicious fruits, there came to their ears the sounds of joyous music and laughter. Then of a sudden, out of the mound they came. I am a serving officer of the armed forces. Sitting in my office is a little man. He is waiting for a reply from me to deliver to my brother of whom I have not heard in many years. I am now going to read to you a passage from the last page. Quote. My dear brother. Hundreds of them came poring from out of the mound. Above, in and around the tree, were so many, I could not count in a thousand years. We saw many little people dancing in the air and playing their musical instruments. In fact, we could not see the trunk of the tree for there were so many. Their sizes differed from an inch to six feet in height. Some of them had wings attached to their backs whislt others floated with out the need of support. Not for a moment could we take our eyes from this spectacular sight. Then, from out of a mist came the king and his queen. They approached and spoak to us for a considerable length of time. In fact. I am sure that you would not in your heart believe was told us. Therefore, I will not force this information upon you. However, I must tell you that we no longer reside in the cottage. I have sent with this letter the chain and locket with instructions. Unquote. The deliverer of this letter is now on his way to his kind, and with him, he takes the letter along with the chain and locket. My brother and his family are now free from the filth that resided on the estate from Hell. May they be happy for all time. As to any proof of my tale. It is on its way to a place that does not exist.

A FAIRYTALE OR NOT

The gift

In Victorian days, people were classed as under class, lower class, working class, middle class, upper class and Royalty. The poor were degraded as the under classes whose degradation was in the Victorian upper classes opinion, largely their own fault; frequently it was said that God wished them to be poor; they were a semi-class of probable criminal tendencies. There was no help for these poor people other than the workhouses. However, most would rather run from these places than enter. Their annual wage was £0. The Lower classes were also poor. However, in the Victorian upper classes opinion had found favour in God. They at least had been given employment, be that it was work nobody else would do for any amount of wage. These poor people received an average annual wage of £10. The working-class were neither poor nor well of. However, they could afford a decent living. These people received an average annual wage of £56.2/6d. The middle-class was not poor but neither were they rich. However, they enjoyed a life most people under their class could only dream. These people received an average annual wage of £150. The upper class were mostly rich snobs thinking themselves better than their lower classes. These people consisted Members of Parliament and those born with silver spoons in their mouths. These people received an average annual wage of £2000. The queen of England received an average annual wage of £60000. William Morgan, his wife and 2 children, lived in an old dilapidated cottage that he had inherited from his grandmother some years previous. Times were hard for the family because they and many others of the era were known as the under classes; I.e. paupers, beggars, criminals, rubbish. The upper-classes, snobs, would have nothing to do with the lower-classes other than to employ them as servants or to do work that they felt not their worthwhile, paying them very little pittance. The only other times that the Upper classes wanted anything to do with the lower classes were in times that war raised its ugly face. The upper classes forced the lower classes into the armed forces, to fight and die for queen and country. In other words, to keep the upper classes in the luxuries they believed themselves entitled. William was fortunate. He at least owned land enough to plant vegetables for his family and would often give much away to his neighbours of who were much worse of than he. His wife Ann took old Mrs Harris's washing in twice a week because the old dear was full of rheumatism and could hardly move around her house. In addition, although the Morgan family had very little money for themselves, Mrs Morgan still managed to supply Mrs Harris with a good hearty meal every day. Television sets were not on the scene and would not appear for another fifty years. The wireless set was a great luxury and never to be found in such a home as Williams. However, he was fortunate enough to own an old harpsicord, and would often play the instrument in the evenings for the amusement of his family, friends and neighbours. Early every Sunday morning, the family walked the twelve miles to the church of St Mary, listened to an hours service and then retraced their steps homeward where Mrs Morgan prepared the dinner after which exhausted; the family took to their beds. It mattered not in the slightest what sufferings the family had to endure, there was always a broad smile for anyone looking their way. When old Mrs Davis asked if one of the children would kindly take the six miles round trip to the post office for a 1d postage stamp, there was never a hidden frown, nor a silent curse, but a smile and

"Yes of course Mr Davis".

When the local tramp went calling asking for a flask of tea and any stale bread, he always received his asking, and more. Late one evening, a stranger called at the cottage.

"Good evening. Am I talking to Mr Morgan?"

"Yes, how may I help you?"

"My name is of no importance. However, many people have told me, that you never turn a man in need away from your door. I wonder if you would permit me a room for the night"

"I am afraid that we have no rooms to spare. However, if you could put up with the discomforts of the small sofa, you are most welcome."

The stranger slept the night on the small sofa and took away with him in the morning, a small parcel of food of which Mrs Morgan had prepared for him. As evening arrived, so did the stranger, and with him was another. "Good evening Mr Morgan. Is there by chance my friend and I can stay the night?"

"Yes of course, there is the sofa and a couple of armchairs"

The strangers slept the night, one on the sofa and one on one of the armchairs taking away with them in the morning a small parcel each of which contained food that Mrs Morgan had prepared. As evening arrived, so did the two men. However, they had with them yet another.

"Good evening Mr Morgan, is there by chance we may stay the night?"

"Yes of course, there is the sofa and a couple of armchaires"

The strangers slept the night. However, before leaving in the morning, they left on the dining room table three small parcels. The first parcel contained £10000 in £10 notes. The second parcel contained £20000 in £20 notes and the third parcel contained £50000 in £50 notes. To their equals, the Morgan's gave plenty. To those thinking themselves a higher breed, the Morgan's gave!

A FAIRYTALE OR NOT

What future mankind

When Nostradamus (1503-1566) bumped into the young monk Felice Peretti, he fell to his knees proclaiming that the young monk would be the next Pope. 19 years after the death of Nostradamus, Felice Peretti became Pope Sixtus V. Nostradamus proclaimed many prophecies and gave warnings to men of the future. He named many dictating murderers although in one case, he did make a mistake in the spelling of one dictator. He named the Nazie Fuhrer of the 19th century as Adolf Hister. Hitler was none other than a sadistic monster who had millions of men, women and children murdered by his evil henchmen. However, when the vile dictator realized that he was loosing the Second World War, a war that he had brought about. The coward shot himself in the head. Good riddance to the man and may he live in Hell for the rest of eternity. Nostradamus also warned men of the future about other monsters. Monsters that would cause the deaths of millions of innocents. Evil men such as Robert Mugabe, Sadamm Hussein, Slobodan Milosevic and many more too many to name. Nostradamus made one mistake in the naming of Hitler. I pray that he made other mistakes. This prophecy is a warning to the people that will live in the 22nd century. In the late 21st century, man will have discovered the machineries for time travel. In the late 22nd century, if a man looks up into the heavens. He will see a silver ship hovering. Slowly loose buoyancy,

A Fairytale Or Not

and descend. The skyship will not be made from the materials that we use this day. It will have been made from a substance of which will be as iron but with the flexibility of a leather gloved hand. It will be built by beings of supreme intelligence. Fortunately for the being that will be controlling the magnificent machine. Not a human eye will fall upon the ship, for if the ship is to be spotted, the being on board will surly be put to the sword. For men of the future will not be as men of today. As the ship enters our atmosphere, the being will look down upon a planet and visualise such sights that if he were a creature visiting with intension of invasion and conlonisation, his species would have all that would be required to live out their lives for many thousands of years. He will see blue rolling seas lapping beautiful golden beaches. He will see islands of lush green fields and forests of many acres. He will even agree that the man made concrete jungles will look to be utopias. However, the being will not be visiting this planet intent on invasion and colonization of his species. He will bring his skyship down and into a clearing in the forest of Sherwood where when he has exited the ship, there will be held in his hand a small object. He will point the object toward the ship and then watch the machine fade into nothingness. He will then

Exit the forest and travel over the island of Great Britain. Unfortunately, in these new times, Great Britian will no longer be an empire. The island will be called The United Kingdom and will be a member of The United Nations. On his journeys, he will note the absence of insects. Trees will be fruitless. He will see no animals on the land or birds in the sky. Rivers and lakes will boast no life. And cities will be empty of all souls. The being will turn his feet to face the forest and his invisible ship however, he will spy in the distance a tower of great immensity. He would know if it contained any reminiscence of the human race. He will visit the structure of ten miles square and above one hundred yards high. He will enter the monstrosity of a building via a small black door that will be located at the top of a flight of twenty steps. He will enter into a hallway ten feet high and ten feet wide. He will not see the ending of the hallway because it will reach the full length of the building. On either side of the hallway, there he will note cell doors made from iron. The measurements of every cell will equal its neighbour of eight feet in length, nine feet in width and ten feet in height. Each cell will contain four iron bunk beds of six feet in length and two feet in width. On the top of every bed there will be a mattress made from straw and one cloth blanket. The final piece of furniture will be an iron bucket for the use of sanitary. On every door there will be a sign, it will read

> GOVERNMENT OWNED CRIMINALS FOR
> INMATE FODDER

The visitor will enter into another hallway and note the sign on every door reading

> GOVERNMENT OWNED CHILDREN 0-16
> FOR PREPARATION

The sign on every door in the third hallway will read

> GOVERNMENT OWNED FEMALES 16-35
> FOR BREEDING

And in the fourth hallway the signs will read

> GOVERNMENT OWNED FOR SLAVERY AND
> HUMAN CONSUMPTION

If the men of the future read this document. They will have had plenty warning. Take heed.

I thank my God that I have been born in this the sixteenth century, for I will be long dead.

A FAIRYTALE OR NOT

Bonnie

Bonnie arrived at our home in the spring of 1985 and was not only an instant member of the family but also my shadow. Yes, she was my dog, a blue merle Border collie. And as all Border Collies, she had a smile that spread her beautiful face from ear to ear and thoroughly enjoyed her games, being dressed up in our daughters clothing or being chased around the garden with a hosepipe etc. She and I were un-separable. In fact, it mattered not where I was; Bonnie was always to be found at my side. When my dear wife and I retired for the night, Bonnie would wait for us to settle before, jumping up onto the bed and lay between us until she believed us to be asleep. She would then sneak under the duvet and cuddle up to me until morning when she would then return to the top of the duvet and lay between us as if she had been there all night. In those days, I was a fit man and employed by a security company. I was given a van to drive and offered a guard dog to take along with me on my travels. However, Bonnie would have none of that. As far as Bonnie was concerned, she was my best friend and no other dog was going into the van except her. In addition, I must admit that my Bonnie proved to be an excellent guard dog. On our first trip out. We had to pick up a parcel. However, as we approach, the guardhouse, the guard did not check to see if there was a dog loose in the van. He attempted to pass some documents through the window. Normaly, when Bonnie and I travelled in the family car, Bonnie was a very placid dog. However, she was now in a security vehicle and knew it. She went balistic. I had only to calmly tell her to sit quiet, and then when after having my face washed, she sat peacefully at my side. That beautiful dog had so much love for her master; she would have willingly given up her life for him. After that incident, all guards kept their distance until I beckoned them forward. However, yobs etc knew nothing about Bonnie and had no respect for neither my dog nor I until she had gone into action. Sometimes we had to pick up parcels from civilian units and once had to cope with a bunch of thugs. I had Bonnie on her lead before exiting the van, however, on seeing Bonnie, they laughed and approached us with their fists and knifes thrashing the air. I gave the usual warning; but they still came onward and toward us with threats of vilance upon not only me but also in their opinion, my pathetic guard dog. Of course, Bonnie went immediately into action sinking her teeth into the backside of one of the thugs. I could hardly hold back my laughter as I watched the yob screaming and very nearly filling his pants as he ran around the garden with my Bonnie hanging onto his rear. The other yobs apparently had changed their minds about us because they did as I bid them, and it was not long before Bonnie had the louts huddled together and waiting for the police to arrive and arrest. Good riddance to bad rubbish. Bonnie had a litter of four beautiful puppies, had we been able to keep them all, we most certainly would have. Holly and Rosker were two balls of fluff and very mischievous. Skipper was the image of his mother and Scampie was the image of a giant fox and just as placid as was his mum. It was very difficult to choose which dog to keep however; we eventually chose the latter and were well pleased that we did. In fact, we very nearly lost Scampie at one stage in his life to a farmer who believed Scampie to be the largest fox he had ever seen. However, that is another story. Holly, Rosker and Skipper went to good homes, which of course left us with Bonnie and Scampie. And, as both the dogs loved to travel in the car, I decided to give Scampie a treat by taking him to work with me one day. However, we were no more than ten miles from home when Scampie decided to jump into my lap whilst I was driving. We very nearly ended up travelling into a mountain of horse manure. I had no choice but to return home with him. When we arrived, we found Bonnie waiting with her tail wagging profusely. My wife told me that the moment the van was out of sight; Bonnie had gone slinking off to the bedroom and cried until she heard the van pull up outside our home. From then on, and up until I retired, Bonnie was a permanent fixture in the van. I usually opened my lunchbox at around 1300 hours and you can be assured, Bonnie was going to have her share. In fact, I could not take a sandwich from out of the lunchbox without Bonnie putting her paw onto my arm and pull the sandwich toward her hungry mouth. It was fortunate that I owned a flask boasting two cups because as far as Bonnie was concerned, she was doing a full time job and deserved the same refreshments, as did her boss, even demanding half my chocolate biscuit of which I could not deny her. On our free days during the summer months, my wife and I would take the family for an outing to the seaside and of course, Bonnie would be the first waiting by the side of the car and ready to jump into her mums seat. We had always to push her over the back with the children. However, Bonnie would not be satisfied unless she had her nose resting on my shoulder and howl in my ear until we arrived at our destination. She enjoyed playing with the children until it was time for the return trip home, then she would gallop up to the car with most of the beach stuck to her bottom. Thus, giving us a good old belly laugh. And although she was the cause of our laughter, she always joined in on the joke jumping all over us and showing her funny ear-to-ear grin. One year we decided to take a camping holiday and so, as not to be tied down with the dogs, my parents told us that they would have them for the two weeks. As a thank you to them, we arranged for them to have a day with us halfway through the holiday. On the day of their arrival, we kept an eye open for their car. As they drove through the campsite gates, there was Bonnie sitting in the back of the car with her head out of the window and howling at the top of her voice. She knew where she was and when she saw us, she tried to jump out off the car window. The moment the car door was opened, she bounded into the tent and onto my bed daring anyone to move her. We decided to break the holiday and returned home that day. After we had packed our car with the tent, camping equipment and the three girls, we were left with very little room. However, bonnie was determined that she was not going home in the same car that she had arrived. So, two of the girls had to return home in their grandparents car of which of course they did not mind because there was more room for them to stretch their bones and most probably, sweets for them to eat. When first Bonnie arrived to us as a young puppy, we were told that she had a short life span. Fourteen years would be the norm for her breed. She was not eleven years old when the dreaded time arrived. Bonnie was outplaying in the garden. I was working in the kitchen and my wife, in the lounge. I heard Bonnie whimpering outside the back door. On opening it, she managed to drag herself halfway over the threashold, lifted her head to look me in the eyes and then rested her nose on my foot. My wife and I scooped her up in our arms and rushed her to the veterinary where we were told that Bonnie was not long for this world. The veterinary saw our suffering and so gave us some tablets for Bonnie with a warning that we would have no more than a few more days with her. Still, we took Bonnie, the tablets and hope home with us. Bonnie seemed to know that she was soon to take her Heavenward journey because when we tried to give her her tablets, she hid behind the sofa refusing to take them. It was not long before we found ourselves facing the veterinary again. I had my arms around my faithful dog and my face pressed up against hers when the needle was pushed into her beautiful body, injecting a lethal dose of anaesthetic. As I pulled my face away from hers, she gave me my last kiss and then went to sleep. Bonnie was born on Christmas Eve 1987. She died at 2040pm 5th July1989. Scampie was born 29th December 1989. He sadly passed away 10.10am 2nd December 2002. On the day that I lost and burried my Bonnie in our garden, I had need to take out the car. Our garden pathway reaches approximately 60 feet in length, and as I took the walk down to the gate, I distinctly heard the usual pattering of Bonnie's paws as she trotted at my side. Of course, since the loss of our Bonnie and Skampie, we have owned and lost yet another two Border Collies. In addition, we now own yet again another beautiful and faithful Border collie. They all have their own stories of which perhaps, I will put to paper another day. We know the spirits of our dogs are with us and that they will not leave this planet for the Kingdom of Heaven until we once again have our arms around them. How do we know? Because there are times when our new dog Bracon is laying at the side of my chair that we hear his food bowl being dragged across the kitchen floor, And the sound of lapping water from out of his water bowl. We hear the pattering of their paws as they come trotting into the lounge. And the sound they make as they lay at the side of the bed when we retire for the night. Finally, the occasional short glimpses of our beautiful faithful angels. God bless them.

A FAIRYTALE OR NOT

Murphy's Law

What is Murphy's Law? Well, let us say that you are walking along a deserted country lane when the moment you want to cross over it, from out of nowhere, there is a long row of slow moving traffic. All week long, there has been a pen sitting on the top of your writing desk. However, the moment you need it, it has disappeared. Anything that can go wrong will. The tale that you are about to read concerns a man and his wife who through death, beat Murphy's law. Frank and his wife Lorna lived with their three daughters Charlotte, Joanna and Petunia in a large house on land boasting forty acres. And of which also boasted a number of coppices and lakes that the family enjoyed. Frank was also the proprietor of a large number of retail stores. There was no shortage of money and the family enjoyed all that they wanted. In fact, you would have believed that Frank and Lorna could have asked for nothing more. Unfortunately, their three daughters were none other than diabolical monsters. Charlotte is the eldest at twenty-two. Next, there is Joanna at twenty years and then there is of course the evil of evils, Petunia at seventeen years. Not one of the daughters will enter university nor will any of them consider employment, believing themselves entitled to remain in their parent's home milking them dry. On Charlotts twenty first birthday, she demanded that her parents purchase for her an Alfa Romeo Carabo. Less than a year later, she walked into the lounge where after a hard day at work. Her parents sat relaxing.

"Mum, Dad. It is my birthday next month. I want an Alfa Romeo 33-2 Pininfar"

She turned to face the door and headed for it. However, before she had put her fat fist to the handle, her father spoke up.

"If you want a new car, I suggest that you get off your backside and take up employment"

"How dare you tell me to get a job, you piece of shit"

"My God, Charlotte, You will be twenty-two years old next month, you have no respect for neither your mother nor I. No man has any interest in you. In addition, you are an ever-empty sponge. Will you ever be satisfied?"

The wicked woman spat into her fathers face.

"What ever I want, I get"

Frank gave as well as he received.

"Not anymore you don't"

Charlotte walked out of the room spitting curses from out of her ugly face.

"We shall see about that you tight fisted git. If my car isn't on the driveway by breakfast tomorrow, I will make you suffer, that I swear"

The following morning the greedy woman walked into the kitchen expecting her breakfast to be waiting for her. However, she found instead an envelope containg an application form for employment at a sewage farm two hundred miles away. She looked toward her mother with daggers in her eyes.

"You have a duty to me. It is up to you two scumbags to keep me happy. If you don't give me what I want, I'll report your lousy husband for tax invasion"

At these vile words from her evil daughter, Mrs Christmas became angry and spoke her mind.

"How dare you speak to me in that manor? Apparently, you seem to have forgotton that we have no longer been responsible for you these past four years. You are a good for nothing and have always been so. The only reason we have allowed you to stay in our home is that we hoped against hope that perchance your heart of ice would in time, have melted. It has not and I doubt that it never will. I suggest that you pack your bags and leave this house before your father returns home. You are no longer welcomed here"

Charlotte just had to get in the last words.

"I'll leave with pleasure but you're going to pay"

"GET OUT"

That evening Frank had not been home more than twenty minutes when Charllotte walked into the lounge and pushed her ugly face an inch from his.

"This morning, your evil wife told me to leave this stinking dump. Before I go, I want my inheritance" Frank became as angry as had his wife and spoke his mind.

"If there is an inheritance for you madam, you will not put a finger to it until my wife and I are long dead. You will now do as my wife told you. GET OUT"

Charlotte was not yet finished and with a satisfied smirk, she declared.

"I told your stupid wife this morning that if you don't give me my dues, I'll report you for tax invasion" However, Frank was ready for his daughter's retaliation.

"Do as you please you selfish woman. I have an accountant that keeps all my records, and I can asure you that they are clean"

Still not satisfied and seething with rage the twenty-two stone, slothful woman tried again.

"That is as maybe but does your fat lazy wife pay any taxes from the money that you give her from your lousy business?"

Once again, her father was ready for her.

"My God, You fat, lazy sow. most women your age would be only to pleased that their parents owned such a business as does your mother and I. Normally at school leaving age, these kids would either enter college and then University. Alternatively, take up employment in their parents business and earn good wages. You on the other hand are a dry sponge ever ready to soak up your parent's hard-earned money. You are an unwanted parasite that will never be satisfied. Have you no pride? Have you no shame? I very much doubt it"

The slob turned her back on her parents and left the room only to re-enter the dining room where she helped herself to a third helping of dinner from the dumb waiter, walked over to a comfortable armchair and shovled the food into the wide gap in her face. Frank worked an average fourteen hours a day, six days a week. Monday, was his day off. One Monday morning whilst he and his wife relaxed in the lounge, Joanna waddled in.

"I have decided that you two can take me out today for lunch and then the cinema"

Mrs Christmas was furious.

"Is that so? Only last week we purchased a MG Sports for you. We also taxed and insured it for you. In addition, we give you a large allowance every week. If you have spent your allowance, that is your own fault. Don't you dare come in here using that tone of voice and demanding treats"

Joanna's face became bright red with rage.

"So you won't give me what I want then?"

Mr Christmas spoke up.

"Your mother has just explained to you that you have a car and plenty of money. If you want to go out to lunch, why do you not take your sisters with you? You have all been given your allowances this week"

By now, Joannas face had become purple.

"Who the hell do you bastards think you are? I am not wasting my petrol because you scumbags are tight fisted. I use my car as I see fit. In addition, I use my money on what I decide. Bloody cheek"

Mrs Christmas looked her biological daughter in the face and wishing that the woman were not.

"In truth madam, we bastards thought we are your parents. However, thankfully we are no longer responsible for you, because you are of age. We are the bastards that will no longer tolerate your behaviour toward us"

The gluttonous woman would not back down but continued to harass her parents.

"Yes well, what about him? What has he ever done for us except to sit on his fat arse all day in his office? Then, when he gets home, what does he do? The old fart plants his fat arse in that chair where the lazy sod will not move until dinner. And what does he do every Monday? The fat blob does nothing. What is wrong with me asking him to get off his fat arse and treat us for a change? Anyway, I need more toiletries and if he thinks I'm using my petrol and my money for these things, he's got another think coming"

By this time, Frank could hold his wrath no longer and gave a home truth to the monster.

A Fairytale Or Not

"Well isn't that just tuff. You are a parasite. You have always been a parasite, and, you will remain a parasite"

Joanna was not going to take, in her opinion, these untrue insults. "I'm entitled to my weekly allowance and anything else that I believe to be my rights, including my inheritance. You are no more than an old fart tin"

Both parents spoke as one.

"You can do as we told Charlotte. Pack your bags and leave"

Joanna had one last sentence for her parents.

If that's what you think scumbags. I hope you rot and die in agony"

You have now met Charllotte and Joanna and no doubt think these two people to be monstrous. However, you have not yet met Petunia. Think of the seven deadly sins and then add a plus. You now have some idea what this so-called human being is. In a few weeks time, Petunia will be eighteen years in age and her parents are desperate for that day to arrive because they will then have the greatest of pleasure in throwing the woman out of their home for good. However, until that day should arrive, as far as the Law, the Human Rights Brigade and the Politically Correct morons are concerned, her parents are responsible for her well being including all the trouble she would cause out on the streets. Moreover, well she knew it. Does it not make you wonder the kind of people that run our country? Let me remind you of an early 21st century man that did not pass his eleven plus. Yet, he became the Deputy Prime minister of the so-called New Labour Party. And then although he tried to disband the House of Lords. The smirking imbecile ended up in the House as a Lords. John Prescott. On her fifteenth birthday, Petunia demande a £1000 flat screen TV set with Dolby surround system. A BMX racing cycle, a Home band citizen radio and £1000 spending money. However, what she found waiting for her in the lounge was a portable TV set, a road bicycle, A Walkie Talkie set and a £100 gift Voucher. A foul-mouthed human ball on legs went waddling into the lounge screaming its mouth off.

"What's this crap? You bastards will get me what I ask for. Or, suffer the Fecking consequences" Thanks to the dictating government of the time, they had introduced a new law. Persons below the age of eighteen could not be held responsible for their actions. Therefore, the parents of any person committing an unlawful act would be held to blame for that crime and punished accordingly. Therefore, for most of this sorry excuse of a human beings life, the Christmases had had to put up with their daughters actions. In fact, Mr and Mrs Christmas had had to call out the Social Services the year before because their wonderful daughter had put a knife in the side of their Border collie. They at least expected the Social Services to warn the monster that her wickedness could not nor would not be tolerated. However, a Mrs Munroe from the Social Services told Mr and Mrs Christmas that they had a lovely daughter and that she would not have hurt a fly. Mr and Mrs Christmas were also warned that if they persisted in making problems for their beautiful daughter, the Social Services would have no option but to put the girl into care for which the Christmases would have to pay. Mr and Mrs Christmas pleaded with Mrs Munroe from the Social Services to take the thing away with them. Unfortunately, Frank and Lorna were to be stuck with the dog-stabbing monster until her eighteenth birthday. Her father was not going to be dictated to by his hateful daughter.

"Greedy, selfish people are lucky to get anything, so be satisfied with what you have got"

Petunia said no more but turned her back on her parents, exited the room and returned to the kitchen where she found her sisters sitting at the table with their faces stuffed with food.

"I'll get my back on them tonight"

"How Pet, What you going to do?"

"You'll find out tomorrow Jo"

The following morning, the sisters were siting at the kitchen table expecting their mother to enter and prepare their breakfast because they were incapable of any form of work. Moreover, when Mrs Christmas entered the kitchen, the sisters burst into applauding laughter. Petunia had swapped the shampoo for hair remover. Her mothers head was covered in sores and completely free from any hair. From out of her foul grinning mouth, Petunia spat out.

"That'll teach you stinking shitbags to give me what I ask for in the future won't it? You bastards"

As for Mrs Munroe, She informed Frank and his wife that they must have used the hair remover rather than shampoo by mistake and that when they realized what they had done, they tried to put the blame on their innocent daughter. On her sixteenth birthday, Petunia demanded a personal computer with internet access and games, a video camcorder, a Suzuki 150cc motorbike and £2000 spending money. However, what she found waiting for her in the lounge was a fifteen gear racing bicycle and a £200 gift voucher. The foul-mouthed flesh ball went waddling into the lounge screaming its mouth off.

"How many times must I tell you slime bags that I get what I want. You will get rid of that shit and get me what I asked for. Alternatively, suffer the consequences. You stupid bastards"

Whether Mrs Munroe from the Social Services liked it or not, Frank was not afraid of the thing that Mrs Munroe believed to be such a nice and polite young lady.

"Greedy, selfish people are lucky to get anything, so be satisfied with what you have got. And by the way, if I was you, I would suck on a bar of soap"

The monster retaliated with

"Well you are not me are you shit house. You wait until tomorrow. I'll make you tight fisted turds regret it"

The following morning, Mrs Christmas opened a jar of coffee and found human faeces had been mixed with the granules. Urine in the milk jug, thin bleach in the kettle and rat poison in the sugar bowl. Frank telephoned the Social Services and explained what his daughter had done and within the hour, Mrs Munroe and a colleague were at the front door.

"Mr and Mrs Christmas, We have listened to your side of the story. Now we wish to hear what Petunia has to say"

Frank, Lorna, Mrs Munroe, her companion and Petunia went into the kitchen and sat around the table. Mrs Munroe was first to speek.

"Now Petunuia, your parents have shown us the contents of these vessels. What have you to tell us?"

Petunia sat at the table looking at the four adults and gave a sweet smile.

"As you know Mrs Munroe, I love my parents very much and would have nothing bad said against them. However, I am sorry that they feel so differently toward me and that they want me out of their house. I really do not want to leave them because I worry so much about them and their health. I am completely innocent of the cruel deeds that they have accused me. As far as my birthday presents are concerned, I am very pleased with what they have purchased. I know how possessive my parents are with their money and that is why I never ask for much when it comes to birthdays and Christmas. I really do not want them to feel obligated to me. Please do not tell the Social Services that they are the guilty ones of all that they accused me. I do not want them to get into any trouble"

All the time Petunia had been speeking; her sweet smiling lips thinned and became a wicked grin. She was lying through her thilthy teeth yet; still did Mrs Munroe believe every word that came out of that vile mouth. Petunia was thoroughly enjoying the discomforts of her parents. She knew them to be furious and that there was not a thing they could say to proof her guilt. Mrs Munroe had been looking and listening to the compulsive liar with a calm expression however, when she turned to face the monsters parents, she became angry and spoke her mind.

"Mr and Mrs Christmas, you have just heard how Petunia feels about you. In fact, she has proven her love by asking that we take no action agains you for blaiming her for your acts of filth. In my opinion, you should both be ashamed of yourselves. You are the most selfish people I have ever come across. Why do you not think that not one of your daughters come to you for help when they need money? You have plenty of the stuff yet, you give this innocent child here a measly £50 a week allowance. You have a thriving business so, what are a few pounds to you? Mr and Mrs Christmas, if I am called to this property again, Petunia will be taken into care and I can assure you that you will be paying a lot more than £50 a week pocket money. Good day to you, come Petunia, show us to the front door"

Petunia and the two women headed for the front door and as they left the kitchen, Petunia turned her head toward her parents and gave them an evil grin. On her seventeenth birthday, Petunia demaned an Audi Coup 2.OL 16V. An ABI Marauder OOD touring caravan and £5000 spending money; however, what she found waiting for her on the driveway was a Mini Cooper and in the lounge, there was a £300 gift voucher. Once again, Petunia was not happy.

"What's that shit on the drive, I told you what I wanted. Now, get the hell out of here and get me what I deserve. Do I have to remind you that that woman Munroe believes every word that comes out of my mouth? If you two shit-bags do not get me what I want this time. I'll make sure you filthy wasters suffer"

Mrs Christmas could hold her temper no longer.

"Think yourself lucky that we have brought you anything you greedy little toad. You have given us a lifetime of Hell. The sooner you reach eighteen years, the better. Because then, we will have the greatest of pleasure in disowning you and kicking you out of our home. Now, get out of my sight"

The detestable girl said no more and did as she was told. She got out of the sight of her parents. She met her sisters in the hallway and complained bitterly.

"I can't phone Munroe because the stupid old cow will say that they at least brought me something. However, I am not letting them bastards get away with it. This time, I'm really going to make them pieces of shit suffer"

She went out into the garden where she found the Christmases pet Border collie Badger laying in the grass and enjoying the sun. She grabbed at his collar and dragged him into an old shed where she found some rope that she fed through his collar and then tied him to the workbench. Then taking hold of an old can half full with petrol, she spilled most of the petrol around the shed and over Badger. She then shut and padlocked the door and set the shed on fire and walked away laughing. The poor dogs agony cries could be heard from as far away as the town. His heart broken owners tried in vain to set him free but could only watch and hear the final wimpers of their faithfull dog as he lay burning to a crisp. They turned to face their evil daughter and saw the vile grin on her ugly face before she turned her back on them and returned to the house. Frank followed the monster into the kitchen where he found her stuffing food into her fat face.

"What foul demon are you?"

"Be carefull what you say to me you stinking shit bucket. You know what the Munroe woman thinks of you. Had you got me what I wanted, you and your shit bag wife would still be stroking the stupid dogs head"

Once again, Frank was on the telephone and talking to the ever-helpful Mrs Munroe. Surely, this time she would take the side of the Christmases. Be-dammed. This time, Mrs Munroe was at the front door with a police officer.

"Thank God you have arrived; she is in her room watching videos"

"Mr and Mrs Christmas, We wish to talk to petunia without you being present"

Whilst Petunia was telling a pack of lies to the two people in her room, Frank showed his wife a handheld tape recorder. His wicked daughter had not noticed her father holding it when he had followed her into the kitchen and had no idea that he had recorded all that she had said.

"Well darling, they cannot ignor us this time"

Petunia and her companions walked into the lounge.

"Mr and Mrs Christmas, apparently you are determining to put the blame on Petunia for all your faults. Petunia has told us that she put the poor dog out of his misery because of his great age and the constant agony he has had to suffer all because you will not spend a few pounds at the veterinarys. Petunia and her sisters have pleaded with you both to have the dog put to sleep. However, you refused. Petunia did the only thing she could. You two should not only be ashamed of yourselves but you should also thank Petunia and not condemn her"

Frank played the tape recorder for Mrs Munroe and the police officer. After the tape had finished, Mrs Christmas explained that firstly, Badger was in the prime of his life at six years in age, and secondly, he was a healthy and happy dog.

"We have his pedigree papers in a locked draw in our bedroom"

Petunias face was a picture of hatred and fear. She knew she could not deny the tape or the papers. However, the police officer spoke to Mr and Mrs Christmas also, with hatred imprinted on his face.

"Mr and Mrs Christmas, if I ever have to call at this property again in answer to a cry for help from your daughter, I will throw the book at the both of you. Your daughter is more precious than your bloody money. Take good care of her or regret it for the rest of your lives"

Three weeks before Petunias eighteenth birthday Mr and Mrs Christmas could hardly hold their excitement. They would be kicking the monster out of their home for good. Two week before the big day, the monster asked.

"If I leave home on my birthday, will you give me some money?"

Together her parents replyed

"No"

At last, the big day had arrived and the monster was nowhere to be seen until there was a knock at the front door.

"Good morning Mr and Mrs Christmas. How very pleased I am to see you again"

It was Mrs Munroe and behind her stood the foul stench and evil image, Petunia.

"What do you want?"

"Mr Christmas. It is me, your social worker"

"What do you want?"

"Mr Christmas, there is no need to be like this"

"What do you want?"

"Mr Christmas, please let's be nice"

"That monster is now of age, you can no longer stick your claws in my back. What do you want?"

"Very well then Mr Christmas. I will come straight to the point. Petunia called at the office this morning, and has asked me to inform you that through all your faults, she loves you dearly. She has told me that now she has reached her eighteenth birthday, you are going to ask her to leave her home. If this is your wish Mr and Mrs Christmas, she will of course do so. However, although you are no longer responsible for your daughter, I must remind you that there will be university expensives that she has not the money to pay. I suggest it would be appropeate for you to give Petunia one hundred thousand pounds. This would not only cover her university fees but that after she leaves university, she will have enough money left to give her a fair start in her new life from home. Perhaps you could think this as part of her inheritance if it makes you feel a littler better"

Neither Frank nor Lorna could hold their tempers any longer.

"Who the bloody hell do you people think you are, Even now, has that monstrosity trying to hide behind you, tells you nothing but lies. She has no love for us, neither has she any respect for you. She is a parasite. She believes the world owes her a living. When she left school, she was offered a college place. She rebuffed it. We offered her employment with twice the average wage. Again, she rebuffed it. How many times have you been to this address knowing in you heart of hearts She, to be the guilty party, and yet, what did you do? You rebuked us. We will never forgive her for her obscenities. Just look at that gluttonous mountain of flesh standing behind you. My God woman, can you still not see the evil in her?" Mrs Munroe was dumbstruck. She could argue no more for the nice young woman trying her best to hide behind her. There was an evil look for her parents untill Mrs Munroe turned to face her. Then, the foul monster put a fountain of crocodile tears on.

"I love them so much Mrs Munroe. I will truly miss them. They have so much money; all I asked was a few pounds. I suppose that I will have to wait for my inheritance"

Mrs Christmas had the last words.

"Petunia, you will get all that you deserve, and that is all that you will get. Mrs Munroe, you and your kind are no more than little Hitler's. Even after Petunia gave no mercy to the poor dog that she burnt and killed, and you then listened to that tape of insults and threats, what did that poxy police officer do? He threatened us. Moreover, what did you do? You did nothing. My husband and I are now going out for a drive. When we return, you will be gone from this place for good. Finally, I have the greatest of pleasure in saying to you and the three daughter of hell, Good riddance to bad rubbish"

Mr and Mrs Christmas left the house and headed for their car.

"Come Petunia, the sooner you collect your belongings, the sooner we can get away from here" However, Petunia was not interested in collecting her property. She took her greak bulk into the kitchen and took up a nine-inch blade. Then forcing her massive bulge up two flights of steps, she entered the bedroom that she had used whilst living as a parasite all the days of her life. Opened the window and with all her might, she threw the blade toward her father who was about to open his car door. The blade embedded itself fully into his chest narrowly missing his heart. Mrs Christmas saw her husband collapse and ran around to the driver side of the car. She managed to drag him around to the passenger side and get him into the seat. And as per usual, Mrs Munroe had no idea what Petunia had done.

"Hurry Petunia, I want to leave this horrid place before your parents return"

"I will not be long Mrs Munroe. Err, I think dad has fallen onto something because mum had to pick him up and I saw lots of blood"

"Never mind your parents Petunia just get your thing together'"

Mrs Christmas turned the ignition. The engine would not turn. She got out of the car and checked the engine. The rotor arm had been taken out and thrown into the bushes of which took ten minutes to find and replace. After fixing the rotor arm back in its place, Mrs Christmas started the engine without more problems. Mrs Munroe and Petunia stepped through the front door and saw the Christmases car pull away. However, before it was out of sight, Petunia produced a brass doorstop and using all the strength in her vile body, she threw it toward the back window. Mrs Munroe could not believe her eyes. "Petunia, you are usually such a kind heated young lady?"

"Sorry Mrs Munroe. That was the very first time I have lost my temper"

"Yes, I understand my dear. You have led a terrible life with those two, let's be on our way"

The nearest hospital was ten miles away and it was the rush hour. At every T-junction, the Christmases were held up. At every roundabout, the Christmases were held up. At every set of traffic lights, the Christmases were held up. If there was anyone that could hold them up, they did. Idiots thinking that they had the right to cross the road at any point, Moreover, when they forced cars to break hard, they did not even have the decency to apologize for their stupidity. Cyclists riding in the middle of the road, and when there was a chance to pick up speed, the moron in the car in front refused to pick up speed but continued to drive as if he was on a Sunday outing. When Mrs Christmas tried to overtake, there was of course, another car coming in the opposite direction. When at last they arrived at the hospital gates, due to a picket line of demonstrators, they were redirected to the rear of the hospital. At last, they arrived. However, could they find a parking place? Of course not, Mrs Christmas took no notice of the sign on the grass verge that read, NO PARKING. She parked the car, got out and ran into the reception screaming for help. Mr Christmas was pronounced DOA. When Mrs Christmas had been advised that she had lost her husband, her heart stopped beating. Not a soul saw Frank and Lorna Christmas leaving the hospital grounds with their faithful Badger trotting at their side.

The reading of the will

To our daughter Charlotte we leave an interview with the taxman

To our daughter Joanna we leave a tin of fart spray to sniff until her hearts content

To our daughter Petunia we leave the contents of the cesspool

To the local animal shelter, we leave our full estate on the condition that every penny is to be used for the housing, Veterinary, food, and welfare of the animals only. Not one penny is to line the pockets of any Executive, Director, or Manager.

Murphy's Law, this time, lost.

A FAIRYTALE OR NOT

Mermaid

There are people living today that would tell you they are living descendants of Sea people i.e. a mythical creature with the head and upper body of a woman and the tail, being that of a fish. As the records show, there has never been a sighting of such creatures also know as mermaids. However, there are many stories regarding these creatures. If a man of the land loved a woman from the sea and she accepted him as her husband, she would take on the appearance of a human being and share the soul of her husband, for she has no soul of her own. She would become a slave to her husband all the days of her life. However, should he ever strike at her in temper, she would return to the sea and be lost to him for all time. I know of such a man and this is his story. Milton had lived most of his young life working along the side of his father, the captain of the Sea Witch, a fourty ton-fishing vessel. He was well liked by the crew and loved to listen to their spine shivering stories of sea monsters.

"Aye lad, 'twas the mighty Baleen Could build city size of London on its back. Aye, had no teeth in its mouth, just washes you in"

"Tell him about the Sea Witch. Aye, tell him about that"

"Why, what's he want to know about Sea Witch. His fathers the captain"

"Not the boat, fool. Sea Cow"

"Many a man been taken down to old Davie Jones locker by the Sea Witch lad. She be as evil as evil be. Half woman half fish be the Sea Witch. There be them seeing the creature as beautiful. Aye, and so she maybe, be you warned lad; do you no good to marry the Sea Witch. Aye, be faithfull to you all the days of your life until you strikes her. Then leave you will she to return to the sea. When you goes a looking on the sea for her, Drags you down with her does she"

Twelve years later, Milton went running into his home with tears streaming down his face.

"What is it father, what is the matter with you?"

"Come my children, sit with me. I will tell you the gain and loss of your beautiful mother. Please forgive me for my stupid temper my children, for it is due to my temper that I have lost my wife and best friend. I have been a fisherman all the days of my working life. One night, as I stood on the deck alone, I was taken overboard by a wave. However, I was not lost to the ghosts of the sea thanks to your mother. Although I cannot remember much about the incident, I realized that the lady who saved my life had to be a mermaid for two simple reasons. We carried no women onboard and there were no other ships in the vicinity. After this incident, your mother and I would meet on a quiet secluded beach. She was truly beautiful as she swam ashore and to me. It was not long before I relized that I loved her. Her tail became her legs and we were married soon after. My beloved children, I heard your mother screaming from the inside of an old fisherman's hut. I ran to the hut and flung open the door. A man was standing astride your mother with his trousers around his ankles. In temper, I went to strike at the monster but unfortunately, I missed him and hit your mother"

As Milton finished telling his children that they had lost their mother, the front door was opened, and in stepped his wife. He had not struck at her but at a rapist and she loved him the more for it.

A FAIRYTALE OR NOT

I will not accept it

Phelps was six years in age when he first became involved in the paranormal in that he saw a beautiful angel. Of course, when he told told his tale, he was not believed. At the age of ten, he met and spoke with his first human ghost. In fact, baring his first six years of life, Phelps has either been physically involved in the paranormal or witnessed sightings in this field of which is of a great interest to many. He was educated at a boarding school of which was some two hundred miles from his home. At school leaving age, he was pleased that his parents had moved home to the famous village of Avebury in the county of Wiltshire because he preferred the countryside than the town. He was also pleased to immediately find employment in the little and famous town of Marlborough in the county of Wiltshire. His hours were long which ment that he had often to cycle home late in the evening and under the stars. The village of Avebury stands some nine miles from the town of Marlourough and the journey gave no streetlights. Knowing this, Phelps kepts his bicycle lamps in top condition and always carried spare batteries and bulbs in his saddlebag. However, one evening, he was three miles into his journey when both his lamps failed. He changed the old bulbs and battries for new but still the lamps refused to light up. He had no choice but to continue his journy home in the pitch black. He had no sooner stridden his bike than he found himself ingulfed in a sphere of daylight. In addition, when he tried to to find the reason for the phenomenon, it was never to be fathomed. Thereafter, Phelps had his sphere of daylight to accompany him home every night until he left his place of employment. On the rare occasion when a vehicle approached, in a split of a second, the sphere disappeared and his lamps functioned perfectly until the vehicle was completely out off sight, then his lamps failed him and the sphere returned. One night, Phelps told his father about his nightly experiences and asked for an explanation. In truth, his father had no idea as to the sphere of daylight. However, he told Phelps that it was more than likely a passing train. Phelps never mentioned the matter again. He decided to look for employment in the capital and was most fortunate in not only finding employment but also accomadation with a wonderful family whose ancesters came to this country from the beautiful Caribbean islands early eighteenth century, as slaves. In fact, it was in the year 1807 that the people of Great Britain made such an outcry regarding the slave trade that the British Government had to illegalize the monstrous trade. However, it was not abolished until 1833. Twenty-six years later. Phelps is a white man and the people he moved in with are black yet, he was treated as a member of the family and never made to feel a stranger. He had been living with Mr and Mrs Hope for a short time when one night he had a dream. Ma Hope was calling for him to get up and dressed. He pulled away his bed cloths and sat up. Farted, and then went over to the electric light switch. The bulb exploded leaving Phelps to dress in the semidarkness. He then went downstairs and entered the lounge where he found Ma Hope and two white strangers wearing black suits. Both men stood up and shook his hand.

"Good morning Phelps. We hope that we find you in good health. We are sure that you have some idea why we have come from the USA to meet you. We are from an organisation known over the world as Spiritualists. Phelps, I can asure you that we are not a bunch of religious fanatics. In fact, we have proof of life after death, and we have people just like you working for and with us in our organisation. Phelps, we have had your name on file for some years now and know you to be a strong medium. What would you say to us if we ask you to join us in the USA and become a member of our organisation? You will be housed in one of our apartments and be well paid"

Phelps sat up and rubbed the sleep from his eyes and the sweat from his brow. He got out of bed and farted, tried the lightswitch without success so dressed in semidarkness. As he decended the stairs, he heard Ma Hope talking in the lounge. He opened the door and saw the two men he had seen in his dream.

"I know who you are and I am not interested in what you have to say. Please leave me alone"

2 am the following morning Phelps was seen to descend the stairs still wearing his pyjamas. He entered the lounge and sat in front of the television set. His eyes were open yet he showed no pupils as he began a conversation with the blank screen. After he had been talking for an hour, he stood up and returned to his bedroom where he fell onto his bed and immediately started to snore. Often, loud crashing noises were heard coming from his room and on investigation; Phelps was seen to be asleep in his bed whilst it was being thrown from one end of the room to the other by an invisible entity. In addition, the curtains were seen to be blowing as if there was a full gale wind in the room. Then of a sudden, the room became still, silent and very cold. Phelps was then seen to levitate a few inches from the ceiling before returning to his bed still in a deep sleep. Phelps was once accused of commiting a horrific crime; he was of course an innocent victim of certain people that wished him to suffer. I will never divulge their names knowing that if ever they read this tale, they will know their wicked guilt and perhaps feel remorse. On that, I will curse these people no more. Phelps knew that if he had been found guilty, it was a certain he would be sent to a place of imprisonment. He had no faith in the figures that sit in judgment in the courts of the land because he had been an innocent victim to a vindictive traffic warden, found guilty and forced to pay a fine. He had also been an innocent victim to a poxy bus conductor who had accused Phelps of damage to a bus he had boarded. Although Phelps proved his innocence, he was still found guilty and forced to pay damages and court costs. Now that Phelps was facing yet another appearance at court, he knew he would be found guilty. This time, he was not going to stand in the dock and look up into the gallery to see his wicked accusers with their smug faces, expecting him to land up in prison all thanks to their filthy lies. Why should he be sent to a place of perverts, murderes and the scum of the human race so that his accuseres could get some form of perverted satisfaction? What was he to do? The only thing that anyone in his situation could do, He prayed to his God.

"Father, you know of my innocence and that my enemies are intent on seeing me sent to prison. You also know that I intend to commit suicide rather than go into prison. I know that when I attempt this, I will be commiting the ultimate sin and that you will punish me most severely. However, father, I prefer your punishment than that of man. I have decided that I will not go to prison for the hideous crime of which I have been accused because there are perverted men in these places who would know me as they would know a woman. I will not be put through this treatment so that my enemies can go around laughing at my sufferings. Please father, if you will not accept my soul, please allow some person to find my limp body so that I can be saved. However, if I am to be found guilty, please take me into your arms"

After Phelps had finished speaking to his God, he waited until the household retired, and then taking up a bottle of extremely strong drugs; he swallowed the lot and walked out into the unknown. A few days later, Phelps awoke in a hospital bed. He did not know if he had been dreaming, however, he had a vague impression that he had been standing in a place of magnificence and that he had heard the voice of his God.

"Phelps, you have been through much. Still, will I not bring you home because you have a destiny to fulfil. You will not be found guilty and you will not go to prison. You will shortly meet and marry the love of your life. However, you will suffer much for your failed attempt at suicide"

A few weeks later, Phelps and his family prepared themselves for the night. Phelps lay on his bed ready for a good read. The bed started to sway from side to side. He called his brother Briggs who sleped in the room next to his. Briggs walked into his brother's room where he saw Phelps laying on the top of his bed and making not the slightest of movements. He also saw and heard the noise of the swaying bed. Briggs ran out of the room calling back to his brother

"I will not accept it"

Phelps is still living this day with the love of his life. For his attempt of the absolute sin, he suffers much. However, he is very happy. Where he resides? I will not say.

A FAIRYTALE OR NOT

Freddie Chambers and Co

The time and date was 2100 hours Christmas Eve 1951 and sitting alone in the officers mess of Tornado Barracks; India was Commanding officer Lieutenant Colonel Freddie Chambers MD. He was a tall slim man with the usual handlebar moustache that for an unknown reason, the officers of the armed forces liked to wear. He was waiting for a telephone call from the maid of his wife of whom had returned to their home in England because she was determine that her baby was to be born there. He had been on nerves end all-day because the last message he had received from her was at 1100 hours to say that his wife was in labour and that he was to expect a telephone call the moment she had had her baby. Sargent Allan Buller, a rather burly man, was standing in his usual place behind the bar.

"Cigarette Sir?"

"No thanks Bully. I'll have another one of those cocktails of yours though please"

"She'll be alright Sir. My Lotty's had four of the little blighters, and still wants more"

Freddie's batman Lieutenant Andrew Brown walked into the mess. A little tubby man with a smile imprinted on his face that all who knew him would have said he never went around without it. He was also the husband of Mrs Chambers maid, of whom was also short, tubby and always had a smile for everyone.

"Pint of the best if you please Bully, Any news from home Sir?"

"Nothing Rusty, I wouldn't be surprised if it's a Christmas baby"

He was not wrong because at 0020 hours the telephone call arrived. It was his wifes maid Molly. "Freddie, you have a lovely baby son. Sally had him at three minutes past midnight, precisely"

1500 hours 27th December 1951, Lieutenant Colonel Freddie Chambers MD sat relaxing in his seat on one of the three Douglas DC6 aircrafts that the army had commandeered to transport demobilized Conscripts. He was looking forward to be home with his wife and new son well before midnight. However, Flight DC6FC became one of the many missing; in addition, the aircraft never arrived at its destination. Five Christmases passed by and not a word was heard from the army about Freddie Chambers Juniors missing father. However, 2200 hours 31st December 1956, there was a knocking at the front door of 11 Redcliffe Gardens, a large town house near to the city of London. In those days, it was quite normal at this time of the year to open your door to thick smog. So of course when Molly opened the front door of her mistress to an unseen visitor, she was none the wiser as to the sight that soon after, she was going to meet.

"Yes, who's there?"

There was no answer

"You'll have to come closer. I cannot see a thing in this smog"

She had only a moment to wait before she saw the strange creature that had brought her to the front door. A hunchback pushed itself forward, however; it was not just a hunchback but also a creature that in all appearances looked to have been assembled from body parts stolen from the grave. It was human; there was no doubt about that. However, it had a large left eye, that was set in the middle of its forehead whilst the right small eye, was set halfway down the centre of the right cheek. The elongated nose had but one nostril, and this was set on the end of the chin. In addition, the mouth was set in the centre of the throat. Whilst the right arm was but a few, inches in length with a hand the size of a large dinner plate at its end. The left arm reached down to the creatures kneecaps, however; there was no hand at the wrist, but a hook like finger. Finally, the creature stood on two legs, one, two feet shorter than the other, thus forcing the creature to stand on an attached stilt enabling it to stand straight. Its clothing was but a grey shroud and a pair of simple rope sandals. It reached into the shroud and produced a small envelope. A whispering voice came from its throat.

"Please do not fear me Molly, Please hand this letter to your mistress with the love of her husband. Tell the boy that he will know me soon enough and that we shall be the best of friends"

Molly took hold of the envelope nodding a promise that she would hand the envelope and the messages she then watched the creature move backward and into the smog untill she could see it no more. She stepped back into the hallway and proceeded onto the lounge. However, she got no further than halfway along the hall when she fainted. Fortunately, Freddie Junior had been playing in the nursery and had just come out to ask for a drink. He saw his Auntie Molly lying on the floor and cried out to his mother, by the time Molly came to, she found herself laid out on the settee with a pillow under her head. Her mistress was sitting in one of the armchairs closest to her and reading the contents from the envelope.

Sally Chambers.

My name is Geratram Chatther. I am the queen in the realm of the Death Walkers of which I am sure you have never heard of.

My Deputy Mr Yont Lairb, will be waiting at the main front gates of Valentine Park at precisely midnight tonight. He will wait no more than two minutes. If you wish to see your husband, you will also be there. Do not worry about the boy; your maid will be there for him. He has five years more before I summons him to my home in the Graveyard realm, to do my bidding. I suggest that you instruct your maid to train the boy well.

G Chatther
Death Walkers Realm"

"Molly, Look after Freddie as if he was your own son. I must go"

Freddie's mother had not even the time to pack a small bag with provisions. She kissed her son and ran out of the house with just the clothing that covered her frame. Neither Freddie nor his auntie Molly was to see mother and truest of friend again for many years. In addition, although the little boy was but five years in age, he had the IQ of a child double his age and through tears, he told his aunt that all would be well, in time. From an early age, Molly had known and befriended lieutenant Colonel Freddie Chambers. In fact, from school age, they had been educated in the same schools and when Freddie went off to join the army, Molly became a teacher. It was only when Freddie Chambers met and married Sally that Molly became part of the family. Now it was definite, Molly was mother teacher and nurse to Freddie Chambers Junior. Freddie was also sent to Mr Pi Chowin, a master in the martial arts. Moreover, thanks to his inherited genes, by the time the authorities sent him away to boarding school hundreds of miles from home, he had mastered, reading, writing and arithmetic to the extent that at the age of ten years, it was not an issue for him to pick up the Telegram and read the paper from front to end. He could add, as does a post office official. In addition, it was no hardship for him to write a three thousand-word essay. Finally, with the help of Mr Pi Chowin, Freddie had also championed Kung Fu, Karate, Jujitsu et cetera. He was defently ready for the world when at the ending of the summer holidays, from out of the blue the Educational Welfare Officers called at his home.

"Mrs Brown?"

"Yes. What can I do for you?"

"Mrs Brown, my name is Mr Spotsip, my colleague Mr Yansem, Doctor Snow, Mrs Summers and as you can see, we have brought a police officer along with us. We are from the Department for Education. We have it, under good advice, that you have in your care, the son of the late Lieutenant Colonel, and Mrs Chambers. In our opinion, we feel that it would be best for the boy that he enters into Bording School. Fortunately, for the boy, we have found a place for him in St Francis Residential School in the city of Birmingham. I am sure you will agree, by sending young Freddie there, he will receive more of a family atmosphere and all the education he needs"

Molly was furious.

"What utter nonsense. I am a certified teacher of the highest grade. Freddie, is a son to me and my husband, for God sake"

Mr Spotsip became very blunt with the woman that Freddie called Aunt Molly.

"Madam, we know that you have not been sending the boy for fulltime education as do we also know that you have preferred to send him for martial arts training. In fact we have had a report that he enjoys showing off his skills on a young innocent boy. In fact madam. Freddie Chambers Junior is a bully and needs to go for special training and away from society whilst he still has a chance to redeem himself. Because Madam, if he continues to use his skills of the martial arts, He will most certainly eventually end up sitting in a prison cell"

Molly knew of the boy that Freddie had had to use his skills on because if the truth were known, it was Kevin Langley, who was the bully. Keving Langley was a thirteen-year-old thug who went around picking on any of the locals so long as they were much younger and weaker than he was. His father was a police constable and his mother a magistrate, and although Molly had no idea at that time, Kevin Langley's parents were members of the Geratram Chatther Death Walkers, she knew of them, and had it clear in her mind that they were no better than was their son.

"I see. The Langleys have made a complaint. Did poor little Kevy go home crying to mumsy and dadams that the little ten year old boy Freddie Chambers had had enough of their thirteen year old sons five years bullying and that he finaly did something about it?"

At that moment, the front door opened and Mr Brown walked in.

"Hello Molly. What are all these people doing here?"

"Hello Rusty, These people are here to take Frreddie away. They want to send him to boarding school because he has finally given that Langley boy a bit of his own medicine"

Once again, Mr Spotsip spoke and this time quite angrily.

"Mrs Brown. Your nethew snapped that boy's radius and sprained his ulna in one strike. We just cannot allow this sort of thing to continue"

Molly was just as angry when she retaliated with her reply.

"Yes I agree, Freddie broke the boys arm, but did the Langleys tell you that therir son and his gang were threatening Freddie and some other small children with their Gurka blades? Freddie had but one choice and that was to get the knife away from the Langley boy. Had he not used his skill, Kevin Langley would have persisted in his torments and finally pushed the blade into the child's stomach. By hurting one thug, Freddie stopped other innocent children from being hurt. What is the matter with you people? What do you intend to do about the Langley boy and his gang who walk around making nothing but trouble for children half their age?"

Whilst all this talk was going on, Freddie had been in the playroom with his new Hornby train set. Mr Spotsip decided that enough was enough and pushed Mrs Brown to one side. He was going to enter the playroom with Mr Yansem and the police officer to inform the boy of their intentions. However, they had Mr Brown to deal with first. Rusty Brown was a gingered haired man, hence the nick name. Now gingered haired people are not known for their placidity, in fact, when they get angry, they get angry. "You maybe some towropes with authority, but you will never treat my wife in such a way again"

In addition, before the police officer had moved an inch, Mr Spotsip received the present of a fist full on the nose which caused him to fly across the hallway and into Mr Yansem who, fell back and into the grandfather clock, onto the floor and flat on his back. Mr Spotsip wanted Mr Brown arrested however, the police officer had need to remind him that it was he who had caused the situation to get out of hand and that there was not a chance in hell that he was going to arrest Mr Brown. In fact, whilst the police officer had been in attendance, he had been listening to all that had been said by all parties. He knew the Langley's and had no liking for them what so ever. His own six-year-old son had been bullyed by the Langley gang so, as far as her was concerned; it was time that the thug received his just deserts. No, he was not going to do a thing about the past few moments.

"Mr and Mr Brown, may I suggest that you pack some of Freddies clothing and perhaps a packed lunch for the journey. Mrs Summers is an excellent escort and will be with Freddie all the way to the school. I can asure you that Saint Francis Residential School is a fine school. I know he will be happy there and, he will be home for the holidays. Two week for Christmas, another two weeks for Easter and eight weeks for summer"

Therefore, before Freddie Chambers Junior knew where he was, he was on the first stage of his journey to his new school and great adventures. The police officer was as good as his word; Mrs Summers was certainly an excellent companion. Mr Spotsip took them by car to Ilford railway station where Mrs Summers purchased soft drinks and chocolates for them to enjoy on their journey. She also bought a newspaper for herself and a comic for Freddie to read. The station was crowded so when Freddie saw the mountain of a man boarding the train that was to take them as far as the underground, it was not expected of Mr Summers to have seen him also. They got onto the train and settled down for the first part of the trip where Freddie watched the scenery shoot by. Station, concrete jungle, station concrete jungle. Manor Park Station, Forest Gate station, Maryland station, Stratford station, Liverpool Street and then down onto the Underground to London and Paddington Station. On Liverpool Street, station Freddie saw the giant again and this time the giant had his eyes on Freddie and tried with difficulty a smile. This was the first time Freddie had travelled on the underground of which he found quite exciting and when finally they arrived at Paddington station, Freddie thought he was in Heaven. Hairdressing salon in the underground toilets, shops, caffees and; trains. There was an announcement over the Tannoy.

PADDINGTON, THIS IS PADDINGTON STATION. THE TRAIN NOW STANDING ON PLATFORM ONE IS FOR SLOUGH, READING, DIDCOT, SWINDON, OXFORD, BANBURY, LEAMINGTON SPA, SOLIHULL AND SNOW HILL. ALL CHANGE AT SNOW HILL. THERE IS A REFRESHMENT COMPARTMENT ON THIS TRAIN

Above his head, Freddie watched the wording on the notice board changing as if by magic.

"Come Freddie, let's get on the train"

They started to walk toward the train when Freddie stopped in his tracks. Twenty yards along the platform, he saw the man, but what a man. He must have been at least seven feet in hight and as ugly as a coot. The man boarded the train and Freddie looked up to meet Mrs Summer's looking him in the eyes.

"Did you see that man Mrs Summers?"

"There are many men on the platform Freddie, Was there anything specific about him that you did not like?"

"I should say so Mrs Summers. His eyes were not in the right place. And, he had a funny nose!"

"Freddie, please do not speak about the deformed as if they have no right to be on the planet."

"I am sorry Mr Summers. I was not being disrespectful. It is just that I have never seen such a man"

As they boarded the train Mrs Summers dropped her news paper of which floated underneath the train.

"You find us some seats Freddie whilst I go and get another paper"

So off went Freddie to find an empty compartment for them and as he entered one, he felt a hand rest on his shoulder. He looked up to see whom the stranger was and gave out a gasp. The stranger had been the very man he had described to Mrs Summers earlier. The man looked down on the boy and spoke to him in a booming voice.

"Do not fear me Freddie; I am not here to harm you, quite the opposite actually. In a short time I am hoping that you and I will become the best of friends because you will need all the assistance I can possibly give"

"Who, who you are please?"

"At this moment in time Freddie, I cannot say. However, I will tell you this. The creature that you see standing before you was manufactured from the flesh of the dead, it is called a Death Walker. The spirit imprisoned inside its body belongs in another. This body was not born with one. I, the spirit speaking to you through this body, do not attach myself to it freely; When this creature returns to its owner I am then imprisoned in the dome of souls. My own body lies on a cold slab in the dome of Flesh and bone. I will only be completely free to re-enter my body when the Hades prophecy has been fulfilled. And I may say with the greatest of pleasure that the prophecy will come to pass in a very short time, then, the evil ones will be forced to partake of their own medicine and may they suffer for all eternity. It is time for me to leave you now Freddie, I have only been allowed to speak to you for a short time to inform you that you and your friends will soon be accompanying me to the Graveyard realm to do the bidding of the so-called queen Geratram Chatther and her gang"

The creature then departed the scene leaving Freddie with a feeling of great expectations. The compartment gradually filled until it contained a number of people that Freddie felt a strong homeliness toward. Then the train departed the station and it was not long before Freddie noticed it gradually slowing down until it arrived into another station. He heard the Tannoy announcement.

SLOUGH, THIS IS SLOUGH STATION. THE TRAIN NOW STANDING ON PLATFORM TWO IS FOR READING, DIDCOT, SWINDON, OXFORD, BANBURY, LEAMINGTON SPA, SOLIHULL AND SNOWHILL. ALL CHANGE AT SNOWHILL. THERE IS A BUFFET CAR ON THIS TRAIN

The carriage door slid open and in walked the most obnoxious, stuck up snobs under the sun. A woman in a light grey tweed skirt and jacket, white frilly blouse, white gloves, black boots that reached just below her knees. In addition, on her head she wore a grey hat with a veil that covered her eyes. Her companion who was no older than Freddie was, believed himself to be highly superior. He wore a white shirt, black suit and tie, black shoes and socks and on his face, he wore a monocle. The woman had need to show of her wealth and importance so spoke in a loud voice.

"Weell Percival. Farst class ooll thar weay. Thar caiptain will oof course be oon haind too eascort us oon a tour oof thar sheep before we teak too oour caibeen"

"Okay yah Mother. Father will be so pleased when he sees us arriving at the British embassy. Do you think he will let us see his office?"

"Oof coos Percival, leet's face eat. He eas thar Breetish aimbassadoor"

"Super"

The train was now moving out of the station with Freddie and Mrs Summers both feeling quite sick. Freddie turned to face the hoity-toity pair aiming his question directly to the boy.

"It must be great going abroad. May I ask what country you are visiting?"

The snob spoke with all the haughtiness he could muster.

"You may of course ask. We are bound for Singapore"

"And you are travelling first class all the way are you?"

"But of course"

"Wow, I realy feel envious. May I ask what ship you are boarding for the trip?"

"We shall be boarding the SS Canberra of the P and O Orient Line"

The train was now pulling into the next station.

READING, THIS IS READING STATION. THE TRAIN NOW STANDING ON PLATFORM ONE IS FOR DIDCOT, SWINDON, OXFORD, BANBURY, LEAMINGTON SPA, SOLIHULL AND SNOWHILL. ALL CHANGE AT SNOW HILL. THERE IS A BUFFET CAR ON THIS TRAIN

Freddie expected the snobs to disembark the train because he knew that the SS Canberra was docked in South Hampton. However, they remained seated.

"Err. Do you mind telling me from where you are boarding your ship?"

The boy's mother looked sternly toward Freddie.

A Fairytale Or Not

"I believe eat ease enough thart you respeact oour preavacy. We are gooing too Singapore too veasit moy hustband oof whoom eaes oof greet eamportance"

She looked around at the other passengers expecting admiration. However, she had nothing but contempt shown toward her and her son. Freddie was not satisfied and persisted in his questioning.

"Oo I see. I oonly arsked be coos thar SS Canberra ease sealing froom Sooth Hampton, ean addition, Oy may aid thait ait this mooment, YOU ARE TRAVELLING SECOND CLASS" the faces of the woman and her son turned bright red and to save face, Percival had to think quickly. "Well if you must know, we are visiting relations before we leave for the ship tomorrow"

There was a young man in his early twenties sitting opposite Freddie. He also, had had enough of madam Toffee nose's self-importance and just had to say something to put a stop to her bragging.

"I see. And where do your relations live. London perhaps? Your husband madam is not the British ambassador in Singapore. In fact, madam, your husband does not represent this great country in any other. As a matter of fact madam, I expect you are accompanying your son to Birmingham as are most the people on this train"

Mrs Toffee nose stood up.

"Yes. You are correct in your assumption sir. However, I am in fact joining my husband at the boarding school my son Percival will be attending. We are the house parents for one of the houses. Come Percival. We are leaving. We are not staying here to be insulted"

There was a girl sitting at the side of the young man. It seemed to Freddie that she and he could be of the same age. She looked up to the woman and asked.

"Are you going into another compartment to be insulted then?"

"Come Perrcival I saw young Christother McGrath in another compartment. We'll join him and his mother"

The moment the door had been closed by the pretenders, there was a great sigh of relieve and everyone in the compartment started to talk as if they had known one another for many years and that they were the best of friends. It turned out that the man who first spoke to the obnoxious woman was in fact a new master heading for St Francis residential school. In addition, the girl was not only his niece but also a pupil of the same school. In addition, there were other children and staff members on the train also heading for St Francis Residential School. I.E. Christopher McGrath and his sidekick Percival Bongtangler. These two were the school bullys, McGrath's mother was one of the two house parents for house two and Bongtanglers mother was one of the two house parents for house three. They, as were their husbands, also members of the Geratram Chatther Death Walkers. The new master was a most agreeable man and well liked by the children sitting in the compartment.

"My name is Mr Reefs and this is my niece June. I will be housemaster of home seven, one of two girl's homes. June will also be staying in home seven. And you young man, what is your name?"

"Freddie Chambers sir, and this is my escort Mrs Summers. I will be housed in home three"

Another boy sitting at the side of an elderly man spoke up.

"I say Freddie. I am a pupil of St Francis and, I am in home three. This is Mr Jacks. He is my escort Oh sorry, forgot myself. I'm called Tony Clark. I do hope we will be the best of friends"

Mr Jacks smiled and then got into conversation with Mrs Summers. The train pulled into another station.

DIDCOT, THIS IS DIDCOT STATION. THE TRAIN NOW STANDING ON PLATFORM TWO IS FOR SWINDON, OXFORD, BANBURY, LEAMINGTON SPA, SOLIHULL AND SNOW HILL. ALL CHANGE AT SNOW HILL. THERE IS A BUFFET CAR ON THIS TRAIN

The compartment door opened and in swayed Bongtangler and another boy. The latter was a little taller and extremely muscular. He looked about the carriage then spying Freddie, he walked over to him and whispered in his ear.

"My name's McGrath. I will be keeping an eye on you Chambers. I don't like people like you"

Freddie looked McGrath in the eyes and spoke in a clear and loud voice.

"You can see me McGrath but you do not know me. If you do not want trouble McGrath, you and your bullies had better stay well clear off me and my friends"

McGrath had never had a potential victim speak back to him. He was going to give Chambers exactly what he needed. A bloody good beating the first chance possible. Little did McGrath and his sidekick know of the nasty surprise awaiting them when that occasion should arrive. McGrath and Bongtangler were in fact cowards and only attacked when they knew that they would get the better of their victims. The pair backed out of the carriage, returning to their mummys and the journey continued in silence.

SWINDON, THIS IS SWINDON. THE TRAIN STANDING ON PLATFORM FOUR IS FOR OXFORD, BANBURY, LEAMINGTONG SPA, SULIHULL AND SNOW HILL. ALL CHANGE AT SNOW HILL. THERE IS A BUFFET CAR ON THIS TRAIN

The compartment door slid ajar and a wrinkled hand appeared sliding it open enough to allow the owner to enter, and as the creature did so, the compartment became cold, damp, and darkness filled the scene. There was also a smell that none could fathom, but a smell so putrid that all in the immediate vicinity felt physically sick. Freddie felt the touch of evil at his side. It was none other than Geratram Chatther. Her cackling voice was then heard by all.

"So, we meet at last Chambers. I have had to leave my home in the graveyard realm because that idiot I sent to advise and assist you has some kind of notion that you will fill the Hades prophecy. I will put you right now Chambers. You will never fill that prophecy. If you want to see your father again Chambers, You will do as I say. I will allow you one week before summonsing you and your perfectic friends"

The compartment was then, returned to daylight, and the monster was gone. Now the talk in the compartment was nothing but of what had just transpired. In fact, the noises of none stop talking, caused Mr Reefs to put up his hand for silence.

"Ladies and Gentlemen, We now at least know where that vile smell came from. We have all just seen and heard the most foulest of all creatures living on this planet. Where this monster comes from we shall soon enough know because she made promise to young Freddie here, that we shall all be apparently summonsed to the monsters home to do her bidding. In the meantime, I say that we continue our journey to our new school and once there, we can form some sort of plan to save Freddies father and destroy the evil witch and her followers"

SNOWHILL, THIS IS SNOWHILL. ALL CHANGE HERE FOR OTHER DIRECTIONS. THE TRAIN NOW STANDING ON PLATFORM ONE IS FOR SULIHULL, LEAMINGTON SPA, BANBURY, OXFORD, SWINDON, DIDCOT, READING, SLOUGH

AND PADDINGTON. ALL CHANGE AT PADDINGTON. THERE IS A BUFFET CAR ON THIS TRAIN

Freddie felt that he wanted to get back on the train and head for home however; he followed Mrs Summmer like a lamb out of the station and onward to a bus stop where his new friends were waiting. For a brief moment, he also saw his giant disapear in the crowds. As for Mcgrath and Bongtangler, a car was sent to pick them and their escorts up for the final part of their journey to the school where, they would be meeting their evil leader with instructions on the treatment of the new boy and any friends he may have made. Little did either Geratram Chatther or her vile recruits know of the teachings that Freddie had not only received but also passed with full colours. Yes, in truth. Although Freddie was but ten years in age, he had every right to claim himself a master. When the bus pulled up Freddie did not notice because he was in deep thought. He knew that there were adventures to be had but he had no idea as the the adventures he and his friends were to have in all the five years that he was to be a pupil at St Francis Residential School for boys and girls. At last, the bus pulled up outside the gates of the school, the occupants disembarked, and as they stood in front of the gates, they could not believe their eyes. The school was massive. Two eight-foot high gates that reached across the entrance were open. Freddie looked at them forebodingly. However, Mrs Summers saw the look on his face and told him that the gates were always open and never closed. The small group of people entered over the threshold and into the school grounds. Immediately to their left was the caretaker's house, this house was most certainly nowhere near to the age of the school buildings nor any other buildings belonging to the school other than the gymnasium and the canteen. The property was large enough to home a family of six. To their right was another building. As large, as was rthe caretakers home but used as offices. This property had been built in the late seventeenth century, as had been all the school buildings other than as said, the gymnasium and the canteen of which had been built not more than ten years previous. Moving on and to their right there was the school playground and four classrooms. To their left were more grounds containing yet another four classrooms. Moving on, there was a flight of steps that led down to the gymnasium and the canteen, the gymnasium was to the right and the canteen was to the left. Between the gymnasium and the canteen, there was also three classrooms, Headmasters office, other offices and the assembly hall of which contained two stages. House

1 homed boys and girls, thirty-two children in all, so you can emagine the size of the property. Each house contained a downstairs Dayroom, Dinner hall and lounge, large kitchen, Ablutions, Toilets, and Office. 'Upstairs' Five dormitories one of which was for the seniors, Bathroom and seniors shower room with toilets. There were also the house parents flat at the very end of the hall. Outside of every house, there were large lawns and behind every house, there was the housemasters' house large enough to take a family of up to six people. There were eight homes in all. House two, three, four and five were boys' homes, house six, seven and eight were girls' homes. These homes were scattered around the grounds and surrounded by fields and trees. House 8 led to a lane known as blind lane of which was approximately half a mile long. Along the lane there were a number of bungalows, these homed teachers etc. In addition, it was along this lane that Freddie and his friends were to find the secret doorway that would take them to the evil Geratrem Chatter and her Synthetic Death Walkers Organisation. Fortunately, Mr Tansley 'the headmaster' was no fool and had placed Percival Bongtangler and Christopher McGrath in house 4. He also banned them from visiting any other house. Mr Tansley was in fact not only the Headmaster of St Francis but also the head of the Anti Evil Paranormal Society. In addition, it would not be long before he and Freddie would be talking for in truth, Freddie was not now just a pupil of St Francis Residential School but unknown to him, he had been enrolled into the headmasters Anti Evil Paranormal Society, five years previous. Freddie and his new found friend Tony Clark were escorted down to house 3 where they were to be treated like a piece of faeces found under the shoe by one of the new house parents I.e. Mrs Olive Bongtangler. The moment Mr Jacks and Mrs Summers had left house 3, the true colours of Bongtangler came out.

"Clark. You know the routeing. The smell on you needs to be peeled away. Bath for you, be off with you, you filthy little brat. And you Chambers, you can wait in the dayroom until I am ready for you" However, Freddie had neither fear nor any respect for the woman.

"I have need of the ablutions Mrs Bongtangler"

"What a pity. You can piss youself before I allow you to go anywhere Chambers"

"You smell as if you have already pissed yourself Bongtangler. I am going to the toilets please or offend you. Bye bye"

Bongtangler was furious and went to slap Freddie on the face however; Freddie blocked the slap with his own hand causing Bongtangler to cry out in pain. Freddie had dislodged the woman's wrist from the forearm and although he had the knowledge to pair the damage to the woman's arm, he felt that she should suffer, as she would have had him. Therefore, he left her crying and cursing on her own in the dayroom. He walked out of the dayroom and down the long corridor to find the toilets. As he reached the last door on the left, a boy of his own age and size walk out.

"Hello, you must be the new boy. My name's Jimmy Bryant"

"Hello, I'm Freddie Chambers"

"Good to know you Fred, I do hope we will be the best of friends"

"We are already Jim Are there any more boys that you think I shoulod know?"

"Core-blimy Fred, There are Loads of kids that you will meet and like. Have you met Tony Clark yet?"

"Yes, Bongtangler sent him to have a bath"

"That'll be a cold bath Fred, Don't let her get to you Fred, I've met Mr Bongtangler but not his wife"

"I met the woman and her son on the train here Jim, I can quite honestly say that I don't think you will like either of them"

"How come you'r not having a bath Fred?"

"Have a look in the dayroom Jim, I don't thing that old bag will be tormenting me again"

Before anything else was said, a boy walked in through the front doors.

"Hello Fred, this is also Fred"

"Hello, I'm Freedie Mea"

"Hello, I'm Freddie Chambers"

Tony Clark came down from a great flight of stairs

"Hello all. What about if we call Freddie Chambers by his surname?"

"Good idea Tony, I don't mind being called by my surname"

Freddie Chambers made many faithfull and loyal friends and through all his adventures, they would always be at his side. Reginald Cox, John Cousins, Billy Honnor, Malcome Wilks, June Reefs, Patrica Patrics and most the staff of St Francis Residential School. House 3 was now full of boys. Each house took in thirty-two children, two house parents and one housemaster. Not including teachers that came in to help. Olive Bongtangler had found her husband Adolf in the kitchens.

"That boy Chambers did this to me Adolf. I want him to suffer"

Adolf did no more but to run into the daytoom where he found all thirty-two boys.

"Which one of you is Freddie Chambers?"

Although the man stood six feet tall and was built like a tank, Freddie had no fear of him what so ever. "I am Feddie Chambers"

The man ran toward Freddie with his arms outstretched. His hands fully open ready to grab at Freddies throat. However, Freddie held his arms out just above his shoulders so that when Bongtanglers hands were near his throat, Freddie brought his arms down forcing Bongtangler to bend forward. As he did so, Freddie brought up his right knee. Bongtangler went flying across the room, unconscious. Mr Brennen the housemaster and deputy headmaster had been sitting at one of the tables talking to some boys when Bongtangler had come running into the dayroom thus, he saw and heard everything. He walked over to Freddie with an outstretched hand.

"Hello Freddie, Sorry I have'nt introduced myself sooner but I have noticed that you have already made a lot of friends. I am Mr Brennen the housemaster and the deputy headmaster, so you will be seeing quite a lot of me. Now, as far as the Bongtanglers are concerned. Would you firstly put Mrs Bongtanglers arm right and, how long will Mr Bongtagler be out cold?"

Mrs Bongtangler was standing at the side of her husband and looking to firstly Mr Brennen with hopes that he would punish Freddie most servvilely, and then to Freddie with hatred written all over her face. Not only did Freddie see the vile looks the woman gave but also so did the deputy headmaster and many of the pupils in the room. Freddie had no other feeling for the woman but hatred however, he took hold of the womand hand and gave a little pull and twist, and it was as new.

"Mr Bongtangler will be on his feet in about ten minutes Sir"

He was about to walk away from the house parents in degust however, Mr Brennen took hold of his arm.

"Freddie, I think you should meet Mr Tansley"

He then called for silence.

"You boys know the routine, Mrs Pickles and the Matron are here should you need them. Mrs Bongtangler, You and your husband will not be required this evening. When your husband returns to consciousness, you will take to your flat or have an evening out if you prefer but you will have no dealings with the boys what so ever this night. Do I make myself clear?"

"But, but. What about Chambers, He hurt me and put my husband who I may add would never hurt a fly, out cold"

Mr Brennen face became red with anger.

"Madam, you tried to slap the boys face and your husband tried to throttle him. What the Hell did you expect of the boy?"

"Respect sir, respect"

Freddie's best friend lost control and in a rage, he told the woman.

"You have to earn respect first you viper"

"That will do Mr Clark, in fact Mr Clark I think it will help Mr Chambers if you come along with us"

Mr Brennen took the boys up to the main school and the headmasters office, Knocked on the door and waited for the invitation to enter. Mr Tansley knew of his visitors and welcomed them most heartily, "Ah, Mr Brennen you have our star pupils with you. Hello Freddie and Tony, I expect you are quite angry at being torn away from your loved ones and brought to this school. However, after hearing what I have to say, I am sure the pair of you will wish to become members of a top-secret organization that not even the Government know about. At this time, there are members enough to count on two hands however, with you two, other pupils, staff members and others that we have enrolled or about to enrol, there will be plenty enough. Tony, your parents are members of our organization. Freddie, your father was taken away from you before you even set eyes upon him, In addition, your mother was forced to leave you with the people that you call Aunt Molly and Uncle Rusty. She had received a letter from a monster of who has lived in the future, the past and the present. I know that you have heard the name Geratram Chatther and, that you have met a symthetic death walker. What would you say if I was to tell you that the spirit of your father controls the movements of that thing, and that Geratram Chatther is none other than a disgruntled politician from the future. The woman died of natural causes in the early 21st century. Her evil spirit was taken into the Underworld where she twisted her little finger around the God Hades. The outcome was that she has control over the flesh of the dead. Thus, the Geratram Chatther Death Walkers. There are now many of her kind. For example, corrupt politicians, corrupt charity chief executives on wages of between £100,000 and £130,000 not including their perks. There are other greedy businessmen and women, for example, corrupt property developers and corrupt Bankers. These creatures from the future, the not so distant future and the far future are evil most foul. Evil people are like wet mud. It sticks. When these evil people died in their time, their vile souls flew directly to Geratram Chatther where they entered into the bodies of the dead and became the subjects of their chosen queen. However, Hades had not thought of his wife the Goddess Persephone of whom he had abducted from her mother the Goddess Demeter. He had not thought that when he had given Persephone the pomegranate, she had only eaten six of the seeds. Therefore, Zeus made it so that for six months in every year, Persephone will remain in the darkness of the underworld. In addition, for the other six months of the year she shall return to her mother in the sunlight and the sweetness of nature. When she and her mother were united, they summonsed Hades to them and the Hades prophesy was born. You Tony and Freddie are here not only to save your parents Freddie, but also to change the future. When you both entered through the gates of this establishment, you saw it as a school. That is as it is ment. However, many doors will take you into other realms and even other planets. Freddie, your mother is working for Geratram Chatther; not of her own free will, I might add. If your mother refuses to do the hags bidding, she will lose her husband to the realms of Hades forever. However, she knows that you are well and that it is you who will be the hero once the full cycle of the Hades prophesy is upon this world. You are looking at me as if you know me and that is as it should be because you also know me as Mr Pi Chowing"

Mr Tansley was in fact an Englishman; he had been disguised Chinese whilst teaching Freddie the skills that he now possessed. Freddie put his arms around Mr Tansley; he had been a good friend for many years. Now Freddie had not ony his friends but as far as he was concerned, a family member. Mr Tansley continued to speak.

"What say you, will you become members of our organization?"

Tony Clark spoke not just for himself but also for his friend because he knew his best friends heart. "Yes, of course we will sir"

"Then you are now members of AEPS"

Both boys looked to one another and then to the two men sitting at the table, grinning.

Anti Evil Paranormal Society, Welcome"

"How will we save my parents sir?"

"Firstly, you must enter into the realm of Geratram Chatther. It will only be then that you know of the Hades prophesy and how you will become the hero that many already know you to be"

"Don't worry Freddie, you will not go alone. You will have your friends with you all the way. Please sir, what about the Bongtanglers and McGrath's. We know they are horrible people and that they will do their best to destroy Freddie Chambers and Co"

"Have no fear Tony. The Hades prophecy is upon us. We will talk more tomorrow. Now be off with you and get your teas. By the way, Freddie, you did right with the Bongtanglers as will you do right with McGrath and his sidekick tomorrow. Never fear reprisals from any members of my staff but be prepared for your enemies"

"Sir, Can I ask why we have been brought to this school err, I mean why can we not fight Geratram Chatther and her monsters from home"

"This school as I have said, has many doors that will take you into other reams plus, we the members of APES must be together to fight any evil that would enter our realm. Now, be off with you"

In the time the friends had been with the two heads of St Francis Residential School, the time had flown by, and so when they arrived at their house it was gone 2200 hours and the boys were ravenous. Mrs Pickles had put aside some peanut butter sandwiches and cold ricer pudding for them before she left for home she lived with her husband in the last bungalow down Blind lane and was usuraly home by 1800 hours. However, due to the circumstances of the day, she remained on duty until 2100 hours. The matron was sitting in the office when the boys arrived. And because she knew the nature of the Bongtanglers, her ears were on the alert, she was up and out of the office in a flash. The moment she heard the boys enter the house.

"Hello you two, Mrs Pickles has left you something in the kitchen. Eat all that you require and then best be off to your beds. You are in the same dormitory as last term Tony and Freddie; your bed is next to Tony's"

There were five dormitories in all; four contained eight beds with the fifth containing four. This being the seniors. There was a bathroom containing four large baths and oposite the bathroom was the senior's toilets and showers. After Freddie and Tony had had their food, they were ready for their beds however, the moment they reached the top of the stairs; Freddie had need to use the toilet.

"We are allowed to use the senior's toilets at night Freddie. I'll wait for you by the senior's room" Freddie put his finger up to his lips.

"Listen, Bongtangler is in the senior's room"

The boys listened to Bongtangler whispering to Benjamin Baker. He was six feet tall and built like a barrell weighing 18 stone. He had been in the dayroom when Freddie had put Mr Bongtangler out cold. He sympathized with the Bongtanglers and was ready to put Freddie Chambers in his place.

"You go on down to the dormitory Tony. I know it is the end one. I will not be long"

"Here they are now Benjamin. Clarks waiting outside for Chambers, Go and teach Clark a lesson first and then give Chambers the hiding of his life"

Baker snatched at the door handle and pulled the door inward. However, Tony Clark was not there, so he took his way to the senior's toilet.

"What are you doing in the senior's toilts Chambers?"

Before Freddie had had a chance to speak, Bakers foot smashed open the locked door however, Freddie had just flushed the toilet and was fully dressed when Baker sprang into the cubical. His ham like fist went flying through the air but it did not connect with the intended target. He put his fist through the system causing his own blood to flow and not that of his would be victim. Freddie's foot shot out like a metal piston rod causing a lot of damage to Bakers patella. Bongtangler who had been grinning until then was off like a rocket and inside her flat. The matron who was on duty for the night had heard the commotion and was soon enough up the stairs and attening Baker whilst taking her report from Freddie, Freddie explained that the Bongtangler woman had been hiding in the seniors room talking to Baker and making plans for an attack on himself and his friend Tony Clark. In addition, although Baker was denying all that Freddie had said, the matron knew Baker to be the liar. In the morning, there was no sight of Baker and there would never be again because he had chosen to leave St Francis Residential School with the help and recommendation of the headmaster.

"I know a liar when I meet one Freddie. You must be dead beat, you can go off to your bed now, Good night, God bless"

Freddie went off to his dormitory and found Tony waiting for him.

"This is your bed Freddie, next to mine. Good night mate, see you in the morning"

On one side of his bed, Freddie had a wooden locker and on the other, there was a metal wardrobe. The bed was six feet long and two feet wide with a straw mattress on its top. A spring mattress was to take the place of the straw one in a few months time. But Freddie had not a care as to what the mattress was made of, all he wanted was sleep and as he lay on the top of his bed he knew no more until the morning when Bongtangler came into the dormitory, shouting.

"Get up get up you lazy sods. Billy Honnor. Cold bath for you and you will have one evey time you piss your bed. Walter Todd, a telegram arrived last night. Your mother is dead. Reginald Cox, Get out off your bed you fat pig. Move yourself Freddie Mea before I kick you up the backside. Jimmy Bryant and Steven Trout, you two can do paper picking around the house lawns before you have your breakfast. And, you two, she looked at Freddie and thought twice before she spoke again. "You two can get washed up and then go into the dayroom whilst you are waiting for your breakfast. Clark will show you what to do Chambers"

Freddie followed his friend out of the dormitory and along the corridoor to the two flights of stairs. Then all the way along the hallway to the washroom, this room measured 20 feet in width and 50 feet in length. There were 32 washbasins along its walls. At the bottom of the room, there was a footbath. This footbath was only used on occasions for such things as athletes' feet.

"You're by me Freddie, your soap, flannel, toothbrush, toothpaste are on the shelf above your basin and your towel is the one on your right. Because your basin is the fourth one along the wall, your number is B4"

Once they had finished washing, they returned to the dormitory to get dressed in school uniform. Moreover, as they entered the room they found Olive Bongtangler rummaging through their lockers. Freddie was furious.

"Who gave you permission to search through our property Bongtangler?"

Although the woman was as white as a sheet, she managed to keep her pose.

"My husband and I have every right to check your lockers Chambers and Clark to make sure that there is nothing in them that should not be"

A Fairytale Or Not

There was no respect in the boys for the woman and they were not going to give any.

"If there is anything in them that should not be Bongtangler, it is because you have put it there"

Freddie approached the woman and although she tried to snatch away at an item she had indeed placed in his locker, she was not quick enough. She knew that she had no choice but to step to one side and allow Freddie plenty room to get to his locker and find the item that she had stole from the matrons' bag the day before.

"It looks like a ladys purse Tony. And it feels full. You can take it out of my locker now Bongtangler." By now, the dormitory had not only its own occupants but also that of other dormitories. And although Olive Bongtangler was seething, for not only did she have a hatred for Freddie Chambers and his friends so intense, but that she also knew each and every boy was witness as to the past few minutes. She grabbed at the purse and attempted to walk away however, Freddie would not allow her to pass.

"Don't even think about it Bongtangler. You will wait here with us until Tony comes back with Mr Brennen"

His friend had no need to be told; he had gone off to find Mr Brennen the moment Freddie had told Bongtangler to retake the stolen purse from out of his locker and was back with the deputy headmaster within five minutes.

"Thank the lord you have arrived Mr Brennen. This boy Chambers is nothing but a bully. He will not let me perform my duties. He says that I have stolen this purse and that I had put it in his bedside locker" Of course, Mr Brennen knew the womans guilt however.

"I see Mrs Bongtangler. Freddie I suspect that you found Mrs Bongtangler rummaging through your locker. This is practice is performed throughout the school every new term because in the past, we have experienced theft by new pupils. Please allow me to appoligize on behalf of Mrs Bongtangler. Mrs Bongtangler, is that the purse that you found last night after the matron had left?"

"Yes of course it it Mr Brennen, I picked it up and was going to return it to her the very moment I see her this morning"

The voice of the matron was then heard from behind Mr Brennen.

"Well, you can return it to me now Mrs Bongtangler"

The matron knew within her heart of hearts that Mrs Bongtangler was the thief and wanted to say as much but, seeing the look on Mr Brennens face, she said nothing.

"Mrs Bongtangler. The matron and I will stay with the boys now, will you please ask the paper pickers to get washed and ready for breakfast"

The moment the woman had left the dormitory Freddie burst out with.

"What the hell are you doing? You know she stole that purse and put it in my locker"

Mr Brennen put up his hands and spoke calmly to the dormitory of boys.

"Boys, we all know that Mr and Mrs Bongtangler are not suited to their stations however, we must keep our sense of moralization. Mr and Mrs Bongtangler have never experienced the privileges that you take for granted everyday. Therefore, will you please give them a chance in becoming good and happy members of our school?"

"Yes sir"

"Very well, those of you that do not use this dormitory will return to your own where you will get yourselves dressed and then down to the dayroom before breakfast"

Freddie and Tony were just about to leave the dormitory when Mr Brennen stood in their path.

"Will you wait for a moment please you two I want to say something?"

He waited for the remainder of the dormitory to file out and then gave his reasons for not taking any action against Bongtangler.

"I cannot talk freely whilst other pupils are present because there are those of them that feel for the new house parents. I am sorry that I had to let the woman go. Had there been an investigation into the theft, she and her husband would have most certainly to be dismissed from their posts and the school. This is something we do not want, you see, these people and in fact, all living members of the GCDWs have been employed by the school. Most of them think it is by the order of their evil queen however, it is not. They have been brought here Freddie, because the moment you perform the act that will put an end to their queen. Forces unknown to mankind will take Mr and Mr Bongtangler and their kind into the very place where they most certainly will not wish to be employed for the rest of eternity. Moreover, that will be an end to it. I wish I could tell you more but I have my orders from the head of AEPS and I am sure he has his reasons. Will you two be satisfied by what I have just told you?"

Both boys nodded to say that they were satisfied in the explanation.

"Thank you boys, Freddie, don't forget what Mr Tansley told you last night regarding Mcgraph and his friend. I will tell you two this though. Unless by the say so of the headmaster, whatever happens on and in the grounds of this school, will never be known by any NAEPs what so ever"

"What is NAEPs sir?"

"The outside world boys"

Tony led his friend down to the dayroom where they met up with Jimmy Bryant and Freddie Mea and discussed the coming fight with the evil Geratram Chatther and her Death Walkers until they were called into the dining room for their breakfast. The room had been set out with a number of tables. Each table had seats for the boys from each dormitory plus the staff table. Each setting contained desert spoon for cereals, Knife and fork for a cooked breakfast and finally a butter knife and jam knife. Breakfast was served up by Mrs Pickles and two other kitchen staff members and this continued for an hour when then Mr Brennen called for silence.

"Members of staff and boys of home three; Some of you may already know of the news regarding the mother of a home three boy so please bare with me when I tell you that one of our pupils received some very upsetting new this morning. Young Walter Todds mother lost her fight to cancer in the early hours of this morning. Walter, I understand that this news was given to you by Mrs Bongtangler in shall we say a way that would not normally be given. I can only apologize for Mrs Bongtangler and ask that you will understand that this lady is not used to the ways of the school. Your father will be here shortly to pick you up and take you home for as long as you need. May I also add that your mother will have the prayers of the whole school?"

Walter knew the Bongtanglers were evil and longed to talk to Freddie and Tony about their visit to Mr Tansley the previous night, and so whilst the two friends were busy putting on their jackets and coats for the walk up to the main school, he approached them.

"Hello Walter. Are you all right?"

"Yes thank you Tony. I just wanted to speek to the both of you about the strange things that are going on. I mean, well, if I just tell you that I am a member of AEPS, I am sure you will understand"

"That's fantastic Walter, but not to sound harsh. I don't think you will be much help to us over the next few weeks"

"Yes I will. I know that you will be summonsed into the queens' realm soon, and I want to go with you. Her realm leads into Hades, and I want to see my mum. My sister was snatched away by that evil witch when I was six years old. To save her, my mother has bean forced to work for the hag. Now she is in Hades. If I can go with you, I will enter into Hades and try to bring out my mum. I am a Catholic and believe that she will then be free to go to Heaven."

Freddie agreed that Walter should be at his side when he was to go to meet the old hag. Then, saying their fair wells, Freddie and Tony walked out onto the road leading them up to the main school. They were just passing house two when.

"Oie You, Yeh You, Jesus"

It was Christother McGrath and Perrcival Bongtangler. There was a crowd of schoolboys walking up the hill. Just as McGrath liked it, He was top boy and the best fighter. No body was going to take that away from him.

"So you think you're Jesus do you, just because you were born on Christmas day. You showed me up on the train, now it's my turn to show you up"

He took a lunge toward Freddie's face but Freddie ducked out of the way. This annoyed McGrath. Nobody had ever dared move away from one of his punches.

"Stay still Chambers unless you want to end up in a hospital bed"

He took another lunge toward Freddie but this time Freddie blocked it with his right arm and backslapped McGraths face. Now McGrath was livid and took a knife out of his pocket. He flashed the knife around and then flew forward with the intention of putting the blade full into his enemies' belly. However, Freddie turned sideway took hold of McGrath's hand and brought it down onto his right shin. The knife fell out of McGrath's hand and onto the floor. McGrath had now a bruised face and a very sore arm however, he was not going to be made to look a fool of in front of the school.

"Percival"

Bongtangler knew what McGrath wanted him to do; they had done this with other boys that McGrath could not beat in a fair fight. he flew down to the floor just behind Freddie so that Freddie would fall back thus giving McGrath the opportunity to dive onto Freddie and pound his face. However, Freddie was ready for this and fell back onto Bongtangler waiting for McGrath to dive. When McGrath did so, Freddie lifted his feet up to Mcgraths chest and threw the bully over his head to fall flat on his face on the gritty road. The bully was out cold, now it was Bongtangler turn. He stood up to face Freddie and smiled.

"You wouldn't hit a boy with glasses on would you?"

Freddie sharply brought up his right hand and hit the tip of Bongtangler's nose.

"You vile little bully"

It was Mrs McGrath.

"I saw everything Chambers. You will be reported to the headmaster and I will make sure that you are off the school premises before the day is out"

There was an outcry from the gathered crowd and then, a penetrating voice of which could be heard in a busy marketplace, called for silence.

"Mrs McGrath. I am a senior in my last term. I also saw everything. If there is to be any expulsions from this school, I can asure you; it will not be Chambers or Clark but the two boys who started the trouble. I will also remind you that there is a no knife policy at this school. I can see that you have two choices. Your first is that you carry out your threat, your second is that you saw nothing"

The crowd dispersed leaving Mrs McGrath to tend her son and Bongtanglers bleading nose. The next few days passed by without any incidences and Freddie met and befriended many new friends. His best of course being Tony Clark and June Reefs, and the three of them never seemed to be apart. Saturday morning, Freddie and Tony were on their way up to house seven where they were to meet June, they were to catch the bus that would take them directly to the swimming pool in the city. However, they had just past by house 5 when Tony got the shock of his life. A Death Walker appeared from out of thin air.

"Hello Freddie, Sorry I did not come sooner, ineverbilitly held back by the monster queen"

Tony had not seen, let alone, met a Death Walker before, so Freddie had to explain his extraordinary friend before the creature could explain his unexpected arrival.

"Tony, this is the Death Walker I told you about"

The Death Walker spoke in haste.

"Freddie I must be off before I am seen by your fellow school pupils. I have to inform you that you and your friends must be waiting on the steps that leed down to the main office block at precisely 2330 hours tomorrow. I will have half an hour to tell you what soul inhabits this body. Then I pray that the prophasy will come true. God bless you and your friends Freddie"

The Death Walker turned 190 degrees and walked into nothingness.

"This is it then Tony, better go to Mr Brennens house and tell him"

They shot off towards the housemaster's house.

"Good morning Mrs Brennen. Is Mr Breenen in please?"

"Yes Freddie. Mr Tansley and other members are here. In fact, Mr Vaughan was just about to telephone house 7. Your friend June and other members are on their way. Come on inside the both of you"

Freddie and Tony entered the house and found it full to the brim with people they either knew or did not.

"Auntie Molly. Uncle Rusty"

"Helo my darling, we've been kept up to date with all your antics and we are so very proud of you. You are definitely our Freddies best friend; Tony Clark are you not?"

"Yes Mrs Brown. We met on the train from Paddington station"

They looked around the crowded room, whom did they know? All their friends were there including other pupils they did not know. There were their teachers and other members of staff however, the likes of the Bongtanglers were not present.

"Come on in and take a seat Fredie, we need to talk"

It was Tansley. He was sitting at the dining room table with Mr Brennen, Mr Reefs, Mr Giles, Mr Vaughan, Mrs Banks and Mrs Davis. There were of course other adults either standing or sitting in any spare seats available. Freddie walked over to the table and sat down.

"Well Freddie. This is what we have been waiting for. I have spoken with your friendly Death Walker early this morning. He did tell me that if possible, he would visit and talk with you before his return to his evil mistress. I presume that he did due to your hasted entrance. We all in this room are to travel into the detestable monsters realm at midnight. It is the monsters believe that we are to become her slaves because she has stolen at least one member of each and everyone of our loved ones. She believes that we will do her bidding or suffer the results of our loved ones destruction. Freddie. You will enter into her realm and you alone will destroy the monster. The Goddess Persephone visited with me many years ago and gave me this"

Mr Tansley handed Freddie a piece of material measuring one foot square.

"She told me that you would be the only person to understand the writing on it, I have looked at the item many times and have not seen even one spot. What do you see Freddie?"

"It is the prophecy sir. It reads. When the hero of a son he has never seen and the mother of the son are taken by an evil queen, the Hades prophecy will begin in that at ten and six years score, the son will arrive in the land of the queen. With friends more loyal, they will not fade away as will the queens. The heart of the queen will be ripped from the flesh; she and her followers will know the true meaning of death. The spirits of the good will be free to begin; the evil dead will serve Hades all eternity. That is all sir. I am not sure what I must do sir"

"You will know what to do when the moment arrives, Freddie. It is now 1600 hours, I suggest that we all try to rest for the remainder of the day and then all meet here at 2300 houre for the walk up to the main building"

Freddie wanted to know where the members of the GCDWs were.

"Freddie. They are all doing, as are we. They are with their queen. She will use them in her realm as overseers. She and her scum are in for quite a surprise"

2200 hours Mr Brennen was in the end dormitory shaking Freddie awake.

"Come on Freddie it's time, you wake those here that are coming and I'll wake the rest of the house"

Freddie Chambers and Co was ready and waiting in Mr Brennens house by 2230 hours. At 2315 hours, the Anti Evil Paranormal Society was walking up to, the main school block to meet with the friendly Death Walker. They had only to wait a few moments when the creature appeared from out of thin air. All Anti Evil Paranormal Society knew that the Geratram Chatther Death Walkers were not a handsome breed. However, they were not prepared for the sight that met their eyes. The creature stood seven feet high, had it not been that he was a hunchback; he would have stood nine feet tall. The head on the torso was twice the size of a normal mans head. The huge left eye was set in the middle of its forehesd and the left small eye was set half way down the right cheek. Its nostril was an elongated slit set on the end of the chin and the mouth was set in the throat. The creatures' right arm was no longer than one foot in length with a hand the size of a large dinner plate at its end. The left arm reached down to its kneecap. However, there was no hand but a hook at its end. The creatures left leg reached three feet and the right leg but one. In addition, on the right leg a two-foot stilt was attached to the foot. It called Freddie to it and spoke so that all in hearing reach would hear the truth.

"Freddie. The creature you see before you is not evil. It is a body made from the flesh and bones of the dead. The soul that drives the creature is the soul of your father. My body that lay for more than ten years in the dome of flesh and bones has been taken and is now cut up to be used as has this body that stands in front of you. This cruel deed was performed by the orders of Geratram Chatther. I know this to be true because there are others like me who look forward to the fulfilment of the Hades prophecy. One of these creatures came to the dome of souls and informed me that your mother lies exhausted at the cave entrance into Hades. It will not be long before her soul will walk into the cave and her body taken up to become a Death Walker. As for that wicked monstrosity Geratram Chatther, she believes me to be ignorant of the happenings that go on in the realm of the Living Dead. This is why I have been allowed to be here. to take you and your friends into Hell. Freddie, when you have fulfilled the Hades prophecy, your mother, I and many others will be free to enter into the realm of our God. Those of you that are here to save your loved ones will have much fighting because Geratram Chatther will be surrounded by a mass of Death Walkers who are prepread to die for the monster. However, I am informed that this is the day. The Hades Prophecy is upon us and the queen has no idea. As far that she is concerned, you are going into her realm to become slaves. Come my friends, it is time"

The Death Walker turned about to face the steps that lead down to the cafeteria, and then walked into nothingness. Freddie, Tony, and June followed and then the rest of the AEPSs. In addition, as they entered into the realm of the wicked queen, they entered the largest graveyard as far as the eye could see. All the graves were open with some still containg their dead whilst others were empty. They saw hundreds of crypts and a monstrosity of a mausoleum. Everything was either covererd or surrounded by plants, shrubs and trees. The enormous Ginkgo Biloba that has a strong smell something like dog faeces, Hedge Apples, Gigantic Yuccas and Holly trees, Yew trees, Peony, Reindeer Lichen, Creeping Phlox,

A Fairytale Or Not

Roundleaf Ragwort, Dianthus, Naturalized Shasta Daisy, Creeping Charlie Dandelion, Japanese Honeysuckle, Poison Ivy, Virginia Creeper, Chinese Day Lily and the German Iris all to name but a few. The mausoleum was no more than a massive brick box with one small entrance in the front. It had been built in the side of a cliff of natural granite, and in the cliff and very close to the mausoleum was a massive cave. Beyond the graveyard, there was a blackness that only the evil dead would know, yet even they would have difficulty in describing. There were many living members of the Geratram Chatther Death Walkers gathered outside the doors of the Mausoleum, some, Freddie and his companions knew whilst others, they had no idea who they were. Entering and exiting many crypts were the Death walkers. In addition, whilst all this was going on, the doors of the mausoleum opened and out came the queen.

"Now I know what that awful stench was when she entered the carraige compartment. It was the stench of rottin corpses. I had smelt it once before, many years ago when I was a small boy. It was when your parents were burried June. However, the smell that came form their bodies was nothing compared to the vile stench that comes from the flesh of that thing who regards itself as the queen"

Geratram Chatther looked to see her slaves and told her subjects to gather them and set them to work however, this was not going to happen. One hundred extremely well trained AEPS ran forward screaming,

"Hades for you Geratram Chatther and yours"

Chatther ran back into the mausoleum and had the doors closed and locked whilst the likes of the Bongtangler's, McGraphs and the Langleys ran toward their enemies Freddie Chambers and Co. As Mr Bongtangler ran past one of the many graves, he stooped down and took up a sword. His first attack was for Freddie Chambers and then for as many as he could take. However, he was one of the first to be put away with a swift sole kick to his knee followed by another kick to the chest and finaly a kick to the jaw. Freddie turned to face his next antagonist whilst his comrades fought at his side. Mrs Bongtangler was next to go. She had picked up a stone that would have smashed a skull to splinters had it connected. However, June Reefs was ready for the attack. She ducked out of the way and then picked up the blade that Mr Bongtangler had dropped and pushed it through the cruel woman's body. Then, after pulling the sword out of the body, she slashed the throat of the womans son, Percival. Christother McGrath had picked up two swords. With these, he decided to show off his so-called skills before his killing spree. However, the flaying of the swords in front of his enemies did him no good because he also flayed his own body and fell to the ground dead. Mr McGrath came a cropper when Walter Todd pushed a pencil through his left eye and into his brain. Mrs McGrath fell to the ground with her own pair of scissors stuck deep in her chest. After all the years of suffering at the bullying hands of Keving Langley, Freddie Chambers was not going to let the thug run back toward the doors in the mausoleum. As the bully ran past his old punch bag victim, Freddie put his right foot out and tripped the bully up. Langley pulled out his old Gurka blades and attemted to slash at Freddies legs however, Freddie kicked out at one of the blades and sent it into his old adversary's skull. Mr Langley had his hands around Freddie Meas throat before being kicked up the trousers by Billy Honnor. The man turned to face the boy that dared kick him up the bum when Freddie Mea and Tony Clark pulled him down to the ground. The three boys kicked the life out of the man as he had done many times himself when a man not of his race refused to give him protection money. Jimmy Bryant sent Mrs Langley's soul into Hades. She attempted to force neat bleach acid down his throat however, she did not expect him to turn the tables on her. He grabbed at the vessel containing the acid and forced the open top into the womans mouth.

"Drink it yourself witch"

The fighting was over. Now it was the turn of Geratram Chatther. The AEPS believed there to be much more fighting now, with the Death Walkers. However, when they reached the doors to the mausoleum, the doors were flung open and out marched many thousands of the creatures. Leading them was the one that was driven by Freddie's own father.

"My son and friends, you have nothing to fear from us. We have fought and taken the queens followers. They are now your prisoners. They are in the dome of Flesh and Bones. The evil one known as Geratram Chatther, We have here with us. The Hades prophesy has arrived my son"

Geratram Chatther was pushed forward and put into the hands of Freddie Chambers senior.

"Do what you must Freddie"

Freddies hand shot forward and was embedded inside the chest of the evil queen. His fingers tightened around a beating organ.

"You once told me that the Hades prophesy would never come about Chatther. Good riddance"

He pulled his hand from out of the monsters chest and with it, he brought out her heart. As the body fell to the ground in a heap, the soul of Geratram Chatther was left still standing. Then from out of the enormous cave appeared half dozen Fire demons. They each took hold of the once queen of the Death Walkers and dragged her evil soul screaming into Hades. In addition, as the Fire demons entered into Hades with their new slave, there appeared from out of the cave many thousands more Fire demons. Within seconds, there was much screaming as the followers of Geratram Chatther were also led into the cave. Following this, the remaining Death Walkers bar one, fell to the ground. The father of Freddie Chambers spoke to his son.

"Freddie. Thanks to you and your friends, many thousands of souls are now free to enter into the realm of our God. Geratram Chatther and her followers are now being punished for their evil crimes against the human race. They will be kept in Hades for all eternity. Moreover, as for Geratram Chatther, she wanted a thrown. Well now she sits on a thrown of red hot brimstone. You will not see us again my son until you are called. However, you have Molly and Rusty as well as your new friends to keep you company. As your friend, Tony Clark said. You are Freddie Chambers and Co"

The Death Walkers body then fell to the ground and as it did so, thousands of good spirits were lifted up into the heavens.

"Goodbye Mum, Dad"

Mr Tansley spoke the last word, in the realm of the dead.

"Felicitations everyone, felicitations. lets go home"

A FAIRYTALE OR NOT

End message

I hope that you enjoyed this book I would say that it matters not whether you believe in any of the tales for the simple fact that the title of the book suggests that you either believe what you read or not. If you enjoyed this short book of paranormal tales, I have many more in my library. Now that I have finished writing this book, my next book concerns Freddie Chambers and Co and of their adventures in other realms. May your God go with you.

Philip Badger Greenwood

Lightning Source UK Ltd.
Milton Keynes UK
UKOW051537060212